HER MOTHER'S
LAST CHRISTMAS GIFT

HER MOTHER'S
LAST CHRISTMAS GIFT

KYLEIGH McCLOUD

Available in e-book and print.

Print ISBN: 978-1-7357192-0-7

First Edition: 2020

Editor: Dennis Doty

Cover designer: Sydney Blackburn

For more information, please visit my website: kyleighmccloud.com

In loving memory of Grandma Shirley, whose love for Christmas and family inspired me to write Her Mother's Last Christmas Gift.

ONE

S he's here! She's here!" exclaimed a small towheaded boy bouncing in his seat. He stopped, his blue eyes widening when his mother took the sleeping newborn from my arms. "She's tiny." He gasped.

"Someday she'll be big enough for you to play with," his mother replied with a weak smile. She re-adjusted the baby's swaddle blanket.

The newly made big brother remained still. He continued staring at his little sister nestled inside her blanketed cocoon.

The children's father chuckled. "What do you think?" he asked.

When the little boy didn't answer, I paused in the doorway and interjected in the family's private moment. "Use the call light, if you need anything."

"Thank you," said the man. He scooped his son up and together they moved closer to the bed. "Ben, this is your new sister, Angela."

Ben touched his sister's tiny fist and withdrew it with a jerk. He glanced back at his father.

His father murmured words of encouragement.

Tears stung my eyes at the father-son exchange. What a perfect family. I want this if Deacon and I ever have children.

"Holly, it's your turn to go on break," said the charge nurse, passing by with a large box labelled Christmas.

The holiday spirit was in full force at the Northern Winds Hospital. Staff chatted and laughed amongst each other to soft Christmas music while they decorated the obstetrics ward. "Hey, Holly, come help," someone said in a raised voice.

"Can't, on break." I walked past and to the NICU.

Through the viewing window, a dozen translucent-skinned babies lay attached to machines that kept them alive. My friend, Marnie, frosted the inside edges of the window. She paused and waved. Her appearance appeared different today.

I gestured at the locked entrance.

She gathered her decorating supplies and tilted her head toward the door.

The door buzzed open. I entered, but Marnie was not there to greet me. Vomiting noises came from the nearby staff bathroom. "Marnie?" I asked.

Someone retched again.

I knocked. "Marnie, are you okay?"

"I'll be fine," she hollered.

The toilet flushed and water turned on in the sink. Several long seconds later, the paper towel dispenser whirred, and the bathroom door opened. I studied Marnie's pale complexion. "Are you sick?"

"No."

Upon closer look, the circles under Marnie's eyes appeared darker than usual. I clenched my teeth and sucked in a breath. My gaze drifted toward her belly.

Marnie wrapped her middle. "No one knows yet," she whispered. "Please don't tell anybody."

My stomach lurched. It's not fair. It should be me. I forced the corners of my mouth to turn upward. "Congratulations."

"If you don't want to get pregnant, I suggest avoiding the water fountain around here," she teased. "I'm like the fifth or sixth person now."

Yeah, everyone but me. I shrugged.

As I followed Marnie through the NICU maze of machines and incubators, she babbled nonstop about her joyous news. Occasionally, I threw in a few responses.

Her incessant talking ruined the machines' lullabies in this tranquil place. I wish she would stop.

Marnie stopped at an incubator. "I named her Gabriella. Her parents abandoned her here, because they don't want a child with complications."

My mouth dried. I will never understand women not wanting their babies.

Tubes and wires encompassed a three-pound preemie who resembled an alien more than a baby girl. I seated myself in a rocking chair beside her.

Marnie adjusted the cords and carried over Gabriella, placing her in my arms. She stepped back. "Such a beautiful baby."

Marnie's supervisor approached. "Mr. Israelson wants to see you in the family room," Dottie said.

"That's strange. I wonder why?"

Dottie fidgeted with the pockets on her scrubs. "Perhaps he's giving Christmas bonuses early this year."

"Oh, I hope so. I'll try to be back before you go on break." Marnie turned and caressed the baby's face. "See you later, Miss Gabriella."

I shifted the baby into a more comfortable position. Mr. Israelson never made us pick up our bonus checks before.

Dottie watched Marnie leave. After the door buzzed, she returned her attention to me and the preemie. "Tell me when you're done with her."

A shrill alarm screamed across the room, sending Dottie into a run.

Gabriella's bow-shaped lips puckered. I stroked her cheek and hummed a song my mom had sung when I was a child. My heart ached. This precious girl's mother did not deserve a baby. If Gabriella survived, I prayed silently she would never learn why her birth parents abandoned her in the NICU.

Someone must have reset the alarm, for serenity fell upon the room once again. Dottie and a male's voice conversed with one another. I presumed she was giving an update on a baby's vitals by the numbers mentioned.

Gabriella squeaked. I repositioned her, but her squeaks morphed into whimpering. I shushed her.

Dottie came, holding a syringe. "Do you have time to feed her?"

"My break is up. Marnie's not back yet?"

Dottie shook her head. She took the baby, avoiding any further eye contact with me. "Are you hungry?"

Gabriella cried.

"I'll stop by tomorrow." I absorbed Gabriella's sweet appearance one last time. What a shame she's not my flesh and blood.

Hushed voices carried through the hallway outside the NICU. Marnie had become the gossip's next victim on the obstetrics floor. She shuffled alongside Mr. Israelson. Her head hung so low that the red streaks on her cheeks were barely visible.

No, it's not possible...

I blinked. The sight of the hospital administrator and Marnie had not changed. I couldn't believe it—she was the best NICU nurse this hospital had!

I gawked behind them as they exited through the ward's double doors. A shiver traveled up my spine at what had happened and what it meant for the rest of us. I rushed back to the nurses' station.

As I had suspected, my coworkers huddled around the desk and gossiped about Marnie's sudden departure. They exchanged theories, though none made sense. My stomach churned at who would be next to go.

Tonight, will be the night, I thought, as I searched through my music collection and selected jazz. I needed it to.

While the music played in the background, I lit candles in the living room. Their flicker reassured the hope I clung to each month. The clock chimed six times. Hurry.

I rushed to the bedroom. Lingerie decorated its bold red color across the bed's navy-blue comforter. He'll fall for this. The eighty-dollar investment would be worth it if tonight is a success. It must be.

My clothes dropped to the floor, and I slid on the lacy negligee. Goodbye one-bedroom apartment.

I struck another match. A thin wisp floated above each candle I lit on the dresser, their glow reflecting on the picture frames' glass. The pictures had marked past happier times. I missed us. Maybe his smile will come back after—no, don't jinx it.

I rummaged through the closet and pulled out my skimpy black dress, Deacon's favorite. He never said no to this dress. Between the dress and lingerie, they would provide a guarantee that tonight would happen.

The alarm clock numbers flipped to six-thirty. Time to prepare our romantic evening meal.

Silverware clinked against the dining room table. I smoothed out the tablecloth for a finishing touch on the set table. Satisfied with the results, I went back to the kitchen and returned with the salad and wine. The clock hands edged closer to seven. Deacon would be home any minute.

Salmon sizzled in the cast iron pan. Two minutes later I flipped the fillets and basted them with herbs and butter, the way my husband liked them. The deadbolt jiggled. I finished the salmon and plated the two fillets.

Deacon staggered inside our apartment. He glanced through the kitchen pass-through. "Is that the salmon I like?"

I set the two garnished plates on the table. "Yeah."

The unlit candles in the center glared at my oversight. While I lit them, Deacon deposited his coat and briefcase on the sitting chair beside the door. He loosened his tie. "What's the occasion?"

"No reason." I blew out the match.

Deacon narrowed his eyes but said nothing. He sat at the table and unbuttoned his shirt cuffs.

I fidgeted with the wine corkscrew. "Wine?"

"Sure."

As I poured, half of the white wine spilled onto the tablecloth. I jumped up and dabbed the growing wet spot. "I'm sorry," I muttered.

Deacon took the bottle. "Why are you doing this?"

"I wanted us to have a nice evening together."

"Hm, I see."

I sighed. My planned evening was not off to a good start.

Only the jazz music filled the quiet void between us. Each time I made eye contact with Deacon, he would avert it. I pushed my food around the plate.

Fifteen long minutes passed. At last I laid down my fork on the plate and rose, scraping the chair across the laminate floor. He still chewed. It became obvious tonight would not happen. I fought back the forming tears. He didn't care. I dropped the cloth napkin on the table with a huff and advanced to the bedroom without him.

I slumped on the bed's edge. What hope was left was dashed when he never chased after me. I shouldn't have bothered.

The suffocating black dress grew tighter. I yanked it off and tossed it across the room with a silent scream. My strategic clothing choices failed at achieving my true intentions. He never even complimented me.

What a waste of money. The negligee's silky material slipped between my fingers. Its charm was lost.

Dishes clanked. Deacon must have cleared the table. My shoulders slumped. I should help. My gaze traveled to the memories that lived on our dresser in photographic form. Our foolish younger selves mocked me. What happened? I gave a sharp exhale at the answer. Wanting a family happened.

Water hissed. Dishes clanged against the sink or countertop. A minute later a cellphone rang, and something landed with a thud. "I promise you'll get it tomorrow," Deacon answered in a strained voice.

Work. I tugged off the teddy. Tonight was supposed to be the night our lives changed. I sniffled, bunching the fabric into a ball. The ovulation testing stick should have just stayed negative.

"What is this?" Deacon asked, startling me.

I threw the wadded-up lingerie. It fell on the floor in a heap at his feet. "What do you think?"

"Let me guess, you saw the smiley face on the ovulation test? I thought we were done."

"We have to keep trying." The air I sucked in made my throat burn worse.

He crossed his arms. "I am not putting you through those procedures again. You turned into a lunatic."

"Please?" I scrambled to the floor and knelt in front of him. Nimble fingers unfastened his belt.

Deacon shoved my wandering hands away. "No."

"Please don't do this to me. I'm running out of time."

He took several steps backwards and re-fastened his belt. "We can't afford it anymore."

I crumpled to the floor, crying. "Don't you want a baby?"

"I… uh… came to tell you I'm leaving." Deacon kissed the top of my head. "Work stuff."

He turned around. "I know it hasn't seemed like it, but I love you."

"No, you don't," I snapped.

Deacon hesitated for a second, then left.

Liquid fire slipped through closed eyes and scorched my cheeks as its salty trail meandered across my skin. My throat constricted until I thought I might die. I face planted on the area rug. Why can't my life go as planned?

I sobbed harder. I wish Mom were here.

Two

I stared at Mr. Israelson sitting behind his desk, unsure what he had said. "What… what did you say?"

"I'm sorry, Holly. The budget cuts are everywhere, not just this hospital." Mr. Israelson pushed a business-sized envelope across his desk. "I'm giving you your next paycheck."

Five years of dedication and I'm only worth a two-week paycheck. The thin envelope quivered within my fingers. "Thanks," I whispered.

"I fought to keep you here, but the board wouldn't listen."

Snot slithered its way over my lips. I sniffed, resisting the urge to wipe it. After last night's disaster, now I had to explain to Deacon that I lost my nursing job. It reiterated his point of not being able to afford the fertility procedures.

A desk drawer slid. Mr. Israelson removed something rectangular and extended a tissue box. "Go home and get some sleep. Tomorrow is a new day."

"Th—" My voice cracked. I took a tissue and mopped the mess, the wet tissue shriveling into a glob.

Someone knocked. "Here are her belongings," said a woman.

This isn't real. I unfolded and folded the tissue wad. This is a nightmare I'm having. I blotted my runny nose again, but it only smudged the wetness farther.

"Thank you," said Mr. Israelson.

A coat and purse dangled in midair by my lap. Are they mine?

"Holly, it's time to leave."

I snatched the blurry jacket out of his hand and crammed my arms in its sleeves. The purse strap slung on my shoulder, I slinked out of his office.

As Mr. Israelson and I passed through the hallway, people stopped what they were doing and gaped with sympathy. The lump in my throat swelled. I will not cry. I repeated the silent mantra. This must be how Marnie felt yesterday during her walk of shame.

The tears floated dangerously close to over spilling. The first chance I got, I darted into the women's bathroom and slammed the door shut, pressing my back against it. A choked sob escaped.

Mr. Israelson rapped. "Holly, you all right in there?" he asked in a muffled voice.

"Silent Night" began playing on the overhead speakers. Mom's favorite song. I wept harder. It would be my first Christmas without her. My eyes squeezed shut remembering our last argument.

"Mom, you can't plan a Christmas funeral. Christmas is over." My pen hovered over the legal pad containing her requested arrangements.

She smirked. "Pumpkin, it's my funeral and I can have anything I want. Now write that I want "Silent Night" sung at my funeral."

"You're not dying yet! Keep fighting."

Mom covered her bare head with a bandana and tied it. She patted the edge of the bed. "Come here."

Tears clouded my vision. I set the pen and paper on the bedside table and crawled in the bed alongside her. "I'm not ready for you to die."

"The doctor said, 'there's nothing more we can do.'" Mom curled her arm around my shoulders, giving a squeeze.

"But—"

"I'm dying from ovarian cancer." She coughed. I gave her the water glass, and she took a sip. "I'll be another mortality statistic."

"Please, Mom. What am I supposed—" I sighed, but it didn't stop the fresh tears.

Mom gestured at the Christmas decorations she had made the nurses leave up despite it being January. "Remember me at Christmas. Now, why don't you turn on the CD player so I can listen to more carols?"

"Holly? Answer me." Mr. Israelson pounded on the door.

The memory dissipated. I swiped away the last tears with a coat sleeve. The bathroom mirror revealed mascara streaks. "I'm fine," I finally responded.

The door swung open cautiously, and Mr. Israelson entered. "It's been a tough year for you."

How can you do this to me? I splashed water on my face and erased any smudged make-up remnant. The paper towel bunched up within my fist.

"You are an excellent nurse, and I'm sure you'll find a job elsewhere soon. If you need a recommendation, call me."

I did not reply. I deposited the paper towel in the garbage and marched past him.

"I'm sorry it has to be like this."

"Don't, just don't."

We walked the rest of the way to the hospital's main lobby in silence. When we reached the entrance bay, Mr. Israelson extended a hand. "I guess this is goodbye."

I glared at him.

"Do you want me to hail a cab?" he asked, dropping the hand to his side.

"I'll walk."

I exited through the glass sliding doors without a backward glance. Outside the hospital, a sub-zero wind gust stole my breath. The cruel negative temperature still left me gasping despite having grown up in Minnesota. When I caught my breath, I pulled up my hood. Home did not seem appealing. I meandered down the sidewalk that led away from my former employment.

The early twilight sky bombarded fresh snowflakes upon the city. I clutched at my hood for protection, but it proved useless against the blustery weather. People hustled by, eager to get somewhere warm. Not me, I wanted the numbness.

Saint Aurora's downtown businesses flicked on their lights one by one, merging with the streetlights. Passersby clung to their shopping bags and children at the street crossing. I lagged behind the small crowd.

The crosswalk light turned green. Being the last to cross, I dashed across the wide intersection just as the light flashed its countdown. A car horn beeped, and I tripped on the steep curb. My hands and knees slapped against the icy concrete. The harsh sting reignited tears.

"You okay?" an older gentleman asked. He took off a glove and offered his hand.

"Thanks."

The lump in my throat reemerged. Worn calluses rubbed against my scrapes as he helped me from the slippery pavement. I clamped down on my tongue to staunch the impending tears.

"You're bleeding." He pointed at the blood smear forming on the leg of my pants.

I brushed past, mumbling, "I'll be fine."

"Miss, wait," he hollered.

I pushed through the crowd. His voice soon blended in with the city noises and people's chatter.

Silent tears leaked down my numb cheeks. The cold intensified the pins-and-needles sensation in my hands. I jammed them in my coat pockets. Through blurry eyes, I searched for the Betty's Diner sign.

The red neon name flashed like a lost long-time friend down the block. Grilled meat aromas permeated the neighborhood. My stomach rumbled. It had been hours since I last ate. I increased my pace as the diner came into view.

Betty's Diner had become my haven from Deacon tonight. I couldn't face him, not yet. I pulled the familiar door, and its bell jingled its usual greeting.

"Be right with ya, hon. Sit wherever," said Cristal, delivering a tray filled with orders.

The diner's heat suffused my exposed skin. I winced at the burning and prickling sensation in my face and hands. Nobody sat in the back-corner booth. I slouched in the booth seat and underneath a flickering fluorescent light. The seat allowed me to people watch.

I flinched at my injured leg's sharp reminder. I rolled up my bloodied pants leg and examined a long, narrow gash along my shin.

"Ouch. That looks like it hurts," said Cristal. She placed a napkin and silverware on the table. "Do ya need a band-aid?"

"I have some." I ransacked through my purse.

"The regular order?"

"Yeah."

Cristal scrawled my order on her notepad. "One patty melt, fries, and a coke comin' right up."

I retrieved my homemade first aid kit from the bottom of my purse and tended to my cut. "Rudolph the Red-Nosed Reindeer" played over the diner's speakers. A child sang along to the age-old lyrics.

The boy sat with a woman, who I presumed to be his mother. She sang along with him and when they finished, she clapped. "Good—"

"Here's your order," said Cristal, setting down my plate.

I lifted the ketchup bottle and shook it. "Thanks."

The little boy sang "Rudolph the Red-Nosed Reindeer" again.

His mother smiled. She helped him into his coat and zipped it. "You ready to go see daddy?"

Cristal gave the customers a quick once-over and sat beside me. "What's the matter, hon? You haven't been yourself since you came in."

"It's nothing."

"Your eyes are red and puffy. Something happened."

Her floral perfume tickled my nose, and I sneezed. Cristal had known me far too long and would pry unless I told her. "I lost my job today."

"Oh, honey, I'm sorry." She wrapped an arm around my shoulder and gave a sideways hug.

The doorbell jingled. Cristal rose. "New customer, I gotta go." She leaned over and whispered in my ear, "Santa Claus looks like he needs fattening up."

I giggled as she walked down the diner's aisle.

Cristal's chirpy voice welcomed the man. The two conversed about the weather and the upcoming holidays. She remarked about his Santa-like appearance.

The man responded with a rich, infectious laugh.

It made me smile. His laugh could make anybody smile, no matter what mood they were in.

He removed his cap, revealing pure white hair.

I chewed a fry slowly without taking my gaze off him. Who is he?

The cook hollered, "One pancake stack."

Cristal delivered it to the mysterious Santa Claus. He asked her a question, to which she responded with a sure.

She went back to the counter and brought out another pancake syrup pitcher for him. Cristal came by my table. "Santa's got a sweet tooth."

I opened my wallet and handed her a bank card. My bill total never changed.

"I'll be right back," Cristal said.

Santa poured more syrup on his pancakes.

Yuck. My stomach roiled at the amount of sugar he was consuming. I shoved aside my empty plate.

Cristal came back, her black eyebrows creased together. She laid my bank card on the table. "Um… your card was declined…"

"It's a mistake." I perused through my billfold, finding only a five-dollar bill. "Let me try the ATM."

I gawked at the written words on the ATM screen. Insufficient funds? I got paid last Friday. How could that be? I kicked the ancient machine.

"What else can go wrong today," I muttered.

"Troubles?" a man asked.

I whirled around and froze. It's him, the man who helped me earlier. My cheeks grew hot. "Bank issues."

"I'm Noel." His large hand weaved inside mine and gave a shake. "Don't worry about paying. I already took care of your bill."

"You-you-you didn't have to do that."

Noel winked. "If you're looking for a place that appreciates your nursing skills, come find me."

"Are you offering me a job?"

"I hope to see you soon." He smiled and put on his hat. "Nice to meet you, Holly."

Noel pulled open the door. A frigid blast pushed itself into the entryway and he disappeared down the sidewalk.

I never told him my name.

"Who was that?" Cristal inquired, holding a steaming coffee pot.

Sharp corners poked my palm. Inside was a small, rectangular business card.

> *Reed's Homeless Shelter for Veterans*
> *Noel Medford, Caretaker*
> *1224 King Road*
> *Saint Aurora, MN 55004*

"Santa Claus," I whispered.

THREE

Deacon's alarm clock buzzed its annoying tune. I rolled over in bed and stretched with a yawn. "Turn it off already."

No answer.

The noise grated. I patted his side of the bed and touched nothing. "Deacon?"

My eyes sprang open. The sheets, covers, and even his pillow had not been touched since the bed was made yesterday morning. I tilted my head for his routine noises. Nothing. I called out his name again.

No response. I shut off his alarm. That's unusual. He never came home last night. I grabbed my cellphone off the nightstand and called him. No ringing occurred.

"We're sorry. You have reached a number that has been disconnected or is no longer in service," an automated recording played.

The phone clunked on the laminate floor. My stomach roiled at what might have happened to my husband. I leapt from the bed and dashed to the closet, flinging open the bi-fold doors. All his clothes were gone.

I backed away from the closet, my hands on my head. "No, no, no, this can't be happening!"

The dresser. I yanked the top drawer and slammed it closed. Empty. The next drawer was empty too. I continued until reaching the bottom, like the others they were empty. He left me.

I stood in a daze. He wouldn't leave me.

Somehow, I staggered to the bed's edge and slumped on it. I panted. Maybe Deacon went on a business trip and forgot to mention it. His empty closet taunted the answer. The lock and doorknob rattled.

My heart beat faster, drowning out the metal's jiggle. He came back! I raced to the living room and skidded to a halt.

Tim removed his key from the lock. "What are you doing here?" asked our landlord.

A brown-uniformed man peered over Tim's shoulder, but did not speak.

"I live here. Why are you here?"

"I have papers requiring your immediate eviction," said Tim.

"Eviction?" I crossed my arms. "My husband has always paid the rent on time."

The police officer stepped forward. "Several notifications were given to correct the situation, and he never complied."

"I never saw them," I stammered.

"Please pack your things. I'm willing to give you one hour," said the landlord. He paraded past a female officer waiting near the door's edge.

An hour? I swallowed. I can't pack twelve years' worth of memories into suitcases in an hour.

"You should get started," the male officer suggested in a gentle tone.

One hour later it appeared like someone had burglarized my apartment. My bedroom had taken the worst hit where a vortex of clothes had vomited across my bedroom floor and bed. Like a ticking bomb, an overstuffed suitcase sat unzipped on the bed.

"Come on," I grunted, pushing down on the lid. "Close."

The zipper continued its protest. I pressed down the lid and tried zipping it again without success.

The male officer grinned at my dilemma.

"A little help here," I grumbled.

He squeezed the suitcase's top while I wiggled the stubborn zipper. At last it reached the end. I released a sigh. That suitcase contained more than clothes, sentimental objects that couldn't be bought.

"Thank you."

"Deputy Pete Belzer."

"What?"

"My name."

"Oh." I tugged the suitcase's handle. It slid off the bed, jerking my arm with it as it landed on the floor. "Ow."

I rubbed my shoulder.

Deputy Belzer walked the length of the bed and stopped at my nightstand. He picked up something. "Miss, do you want this?"

"Don't touch my stuff." I plucked it out of his hand. It was the business card I had gotten yesterday. I stuffed it, along with my cellphone, inside my purse.

"Do you want me to take your suitcase?"

"I can do it myself."

I pulled up the handle and rolled it, but the wheels did not work under the suitcase's heavy load. The monstrous suitcase would not budge. I let out a growl,

Deputy Belzer chuckled. "Stop. I'll carry it."

"Thanks. I'll meet you downstairs."

The female deputy followed as I strolled through the apartment one last time. Satisfied that I didn't miss anything, I put on my jacket and grabbed my purse. I paused in the doorway. Deacon and I had lived here for twelve years, the only home we shared. Within the same day, I had lost both my husband and my home.

"Time to leave," said the woman.

Goodbye. I locked the door to my apartment and handed her my set of keys.

Deputy Belzer waited by the apartment building's mailboxes in the front entry. He straightened upon seeing me and his partner. "Do you have somewhere to go to?"

"N-n-o-o," I croaked, catching my bottom lip with my teeth.

"Would you like a ride?"

"Please."

Deputy Belzer led us outside to where the squad car was parked. He lifted the suitcase into the trunk like it weighed nothing while his partner opened the back door.

I felt like a criminal climbing in the backseat. The steel mesh cage, that separated us, seemed to box me in further. My heart beat faster. I... I can't breathe.

"Where to?" asked Deputy Belzer.

"How long before I can report someone missing?"

"Why? Who do you think is missing?"

"My husband. He never came home last night, and when I call his phone, it keeps saying the number's been disconnected." I met his gaze in the rear-view mirror.

"Are his things still there?"

"No."

His lips pursed. "Any marital problems?"

I shook my head. Not that I would tell you. "Could you take me to Hollis and Wood Law Office? I'd like to see if my husband showed up for work."

"Yeah, we can do that." Deputy Belzer held the radio to his mouth. "We'll go in a minute. I have to report first."

Deputy Belzer parked the squad car in front of Hollis and Wood Law Office. He darted around the vehicle and opened my locked door. As I got out, he spoke, "We'll wait for you in case he's not here."

"It should take only a minute."

I entered the attorneys' office that Deacon had worked at for over a decade. No one waited in line at the metal detector. I stopped at the conveyor belt.

"Holly," Willie, the building's security guard stated. His soft brown eyes reflected my disheveled appearance. "Deacon no longer works here."

"What? No, you're lying." I marched through the metal detector, causing multiple shrill beeps.

"You can't go up there."

Thick arms restrained me in front of the elevator. I squirmed. "Let me go. He has to be here."

"He quit yesterday."

"Deacon," I shouted.

"I'm sorry, but he's not here."

It's true. Deacon left me. A heaviness fell upon my body at the realization Deacon had planned it. He should have told me.

Willie released his hold. "Divorce was tough on me too."

"Divorce?" I collapsed on the bench beside the elevator. A slow burn wound itself into a tighter knot in my chest. After twelve years of marriage, he's gone just like that—no goodbyes, no 'I'm sorry?'

"You'll get through this." Willie kneeled. "Deacon left you a package at my desk."

"Oh." I didn't know how else to respond.

Willie herded me back to the metal detector. A thick packet with my name written on it lay on top of his desk. He picked it up and held it out.

I grabbed it and fled the building.

The woman deputy leaned against the car while talking with Deputy Belzer. She glanced at me. "Not there, huh?"

"I don't want to talk about it." I wrenched the car handle and plopped in the backseat.

"Ma'am, is there anywhere else you can go?" asked Deputy Belzer.

"No... I don't have anyone else." I stifled a sob. It was no use, sob after sob burst out. I interlaced my fingers in the cage holes and pressed my forehead against the cool metal, holding it there.

"What about that shelter on the business card?"

"I'm... uh... not a veteran."

"Noel's worked a few miracles," said Deputy Belzer. He started the car and shifted it into drive without waiting for my reply.

I dried my face. "You know him?"

"His son and I served in the same battalion in Iraq three tours." The blinker signal clicked, and Deputy Belzer swiveled the steering wheel to the right. "Noel and I met at Reed's funeral."

The homeless shelter was named in memory of his son. I wanted to ask how Noel's son died but didn't. I looked out the window instead.

Silent questions swarmed around my head about my predicament. An ache formed behind my eyes. The radio's chatter aggravated my tension headache and massaging did not relieve it. My eyelids fluttered shut.

The car slowed. "We're here," said Deputy Belzer.

Naked trees lined the front of the property's fence. As we drove past them, the facility came into a clearer view. It perhaps had been an institution at one time or a mansion that had additional wings built over the years.

Withered brown vines clung to the façade despite being battered by the wind. The two columns outside the shelter's front doors displayed deep cracks. Deputy Belzer parked the car. "I'll get your suitcase."

His partner freed me from my prison, and I wasted no time getting out. I raised the metal knocker on the shelter's door.

"Don't," said Deputy Belzer. He twisted the knob and walked in without an invitation.

Inside was a massive foyer that could fit a large receiving party. I gawked at the sheer height of the vaulted ceiling that hovered above. Deputy Belzer gestured at a room with partitioned walls. "That's the office."

Santa—I mean Noel—rose from his chair with a smile. "Holly, I thought we'd see you today. Thank you, Pete, for delivering her here."

Pete saluted. He placed my suitcase by Noel's desk. As he was leaving, he whispered in my ear, "Don't worry, you're in good hands here with Noel."

I swallowed what little spit I had in my mouth. My stomach announced its unfed state, bringing warmth to my face.

"I'm hungry for pancakes. How about you?" asked Noel.

"Pancakes sound good." I feigned a smile. Ugh, I would have anything but pancakes.

"You can leave your suitcase here. I'll have a man bring it to your room." He rubbed his palms together. "Let's go get us some pancakes."

"How do you know my name?"

"Santa Claus knows everyone." Noel winked. "We better hurry while the kitchen is free."

Men and occasionally a woman gaped as we passed them in what Noel called the lobby. We turned left into a hallway when Noel spoke, "the women stay on the upper levels. You'll see more down here around lunch and the afternoon when they have their support group."

"There are homeless women veterans?"

"According to statistics, their numbers are rising." Noel swung open a door that revealed an enormous kitchen. A mischievous twinkle brightened his hazel eyes.

"We best hurry before the cooks come in to start the noon meal."

He whipped the pancake batter with ease. The griddle crackled as he spooned ten round circles on it.

"Are you sure I can stay here? I'm not a veteran."

"Your people skills will make up for you not being a veteran." Noel flicked his wrist, flipping the pancakes. When he finished, he went to the industrial-sized refrigerator and pulled out a bowl containing cut-up strawberries.

I tilted my head. "How did—"

"Syrup makes you sick, right?"

Noel placed the bowl on the counter and pulled two plates from the cupboard. He stacked five pancakes on each. "Breakfast is served."

"Thanks. I didn't get to eat this morning." I topped the pancakes with the strawberries and its juice.

Like at Betty's Diner, Noel bathed his pancakes with maple syrup. "I'm sorry you had a rough morning. After we finish eating, would you like a tour of the place?"

"To be honest Noel, I would rather go to my room."

"Understandable."

"I had a terrible couple of days."

"Your husband leave ya?" Sticky syrup clung to Noel's white beard. He wet his napkin and wiped his beard, leaving behind pieces of the napkin. "Man like that is a coward. You deserve better than him."

I stared at him. If he knew about Deacon leaving me, maybe he really was Santa.

Four

The fragrance of brewing coffee wafted into my room. It was still dark outside. I pressed a random button on my cellphone and the screen illuminated four-thirty a.m. Coffee. Need coffee.

I slipped on my polka-dotted bathrobe and snuck out of my shared room, following the coffee aroma into a lounge. Inside, a pregnant woman sat in a chair with her feet up on the coffee table. Her hands cradled a foam cup filled with black coffee.

"Are you the one with the good smelling coffee?" I asked, "Is there more?"

She pointed at the coffeepot. "Help yourself."

I dumped a substantial amount of powdered creamer on the cup's bottom and added my favorite liquid. The cream and coffee swirled with one another, settling on a pale-brown color. I took a sip. "Mmm. Nothing like a cup of coffee to touch your soul in the morning."

"I ain't ever heard that before." The woman gave a partial smile.

"Holly Bradford."

"Chloe Robinson."

I stared at her baby bump. Her swollen abdomen bulged past the sweatshirt's maximum stretch, leaving exposed skin. It had been ten years since Deacon and I had tried to get pregnant.

"I'm sorry, you have what's called unexplained infertility," said the fertility specialist.

"What does that mean?" asked Deacon.

"We don't know why Holly's not getting pregnant. Both of your test results are fine so you should be able to get pregnant."

"There… there must be more we can do." I wrung and re-wrung my hands in my lap, unable to look at his face.

Chloe intruded on my despair. "Well?" She tugged her shirt down farther.

"Well what?"

"Aren't you gonna ask when I'm due?"

"No."

"Good. People don't understand about this baby." Her voice came out hard. "It should have never happened."

She must have been a rape victim and the baby a resulting product from her trauma, or she had a one-night stand and got pregnant by accident. It's not fair. Chloe didn't even want a baby, and she got one.

"You the new nurse?"

"Yeah."

"What branch did you serve?"

"I didn't. Noel invited me here."

Chloe rose from her seat, her brown eyes narrowed into slits. She stretched like a cat that had lazed too long. "Word of advice, we don't like outsiders here."

"Wh—"

Chloe waddled out, leaving me behind with an unanswered question.

I swallowed the last of my coffee and headed to the showers I had found three doors down.

The lukewarm water trickled downward. I reflected upon Deacon's past behavior. All those late nights... he must have left me for another woman, one that could have babies. I had missed the signs.

That unopened package contained the answers. I couldn't do it. I clenched my jaw at the contents it contained. How could somebody be married to you for twelve years and vanish out of your life overnight without warning? Who tells somebody they want a divorce through a package? I balled up a fist and brought it to the shower tile.

When the water grew cold, I turned off the faucet and dried myself, including the tears. The tepid water did not loosen my tense muscles.

I slipped back into my room and dressed in-between my roommate's snores. Let's see if I can find the kitchen.

A faint odor cloyed the air in the hallway, and I wrinkled my nose. Ugh, this is the men's floor. I retraced my steps to find the elevator. "I need more coffee," I muttered, "can't believe I got off on the wrong floor."

A man, without a shirt, emerged into my path. He stretched his arms above his head and let out a loud yawn.

"Excuse me. Can you tell me where the kitchen is?" I asked.

His black hair was twisted in a man bun. When he turned, I gasped at the white scars that peppered the right side of his body.

An elevator dinged down the hallway and heavy footsteps entered.

The man clamped my wrist and pulled me into a dim room. He pressed my back against a wall. "Shhh... you need to work on your shock. There are others here with scars far worse than mine."

"Let—"

"I'm sorry." The man planted his lips on mine.

I squealed and pushed at his chest, but it only made him kiss harder. Candied orange infused my mouth.

Hands cupped my face. His flavored tongue tantalized mine with its swirls, like they were two dancers. A slow tingle rippled across my nerve endings. The man's stubbled jaw heightened the feeling with each prickle.

I returned the kisses, wanting—no, needing more.

"Christian? I saw you go in here," said a gravelly voice.

Christian replaced his lips with a hand. He glanced at the man, his nose brushing against mine. "Can't you see I'm busy?"

"Noel's looking for you." As the man turned, puckered skin glistened under the hallway lights.

"Tell the old man I'll be right there."

The man mumbled something as he walked away.

"You must be Holly." Christian removed his hand. He leaned his lips close enough where he might kiss me again. "Rule number one, you don't go anywhere in this building without an escort."

He snagged a shirt off a chair beside us and pulled it over his head. "I'll take ya to Noel."

"Where are we anyway?"

"My room. Why? Did you want to finish making out?" Christian gave a semi-grin. "Stick close."

Warmth crept into my face.

Christian's breath tickled behind my ear as he whispered, "Maybe later."

The heat shifted to my armpits. Stop it. It was just a harmless kiss for distraction.

Noel and a woman argued in the lobby. "Come on, Noel. I promise I'll stay clean this time," she pleaded.

"Leila, I'm sorry, but you broke the rules. Take your bag and go." Noel waved over a guard.

"Don't bother," Leila snapped. "I'll walk myself out."

The guard followed her outside.

"That woman," I trailed off.

"Don't worry about Leila. She's tough as nails," said Christian. "She'll be back."

"Why did you make her leave?"

"When veterans stay with us, they can't drink or do drugs, and they have to follow our midnight curfew. If they don't, then we kick them out. It's tough, but we have to do it to maintain order," Noel explained.

"I don't know about you two, but I'm starving." Christian's nostrils flared. "Smells like bacon today."

Noel and I ambled behind Christian. "This place is not affiliated with the VA. As long as the donations keep coming in, we'll stay open," said Noel.

"Will I get paid?"

"All positions are volunteer work."

"I need a job."

We entered through the kitchen door. All chatter ceased, and a group of people looked at me. Christian curled his fingers around my shoulders. "This is Holly. She'll work with me in the infirmary."

He pulled out an empty chair which belonged to an oak table that seated twelve. A spread of platters and bowls containing various breakfast foods sat in the table's middle, waiting to be eaten by what seemed like an army in the kitchen.

Christian provided introductions. They created an easy camaraderie with one another throughout our meal.

This is what a family must feel like. A sniffle threatened a full-fledged sob at what I had lost.

"Whatcha thinkin' about?" Christian asked in a hushed tone.

"Please excuse me." I got up from the table and darted out of the kitchen.

The lump in my throat squeezed tighter. The faster I walked, the more my shoes clacked against the hallway's flooring. Blurred people passed by, moving out of the way.

"Holly, stop. Wait."

The door to every room was closed. I finally selected one to escape from Christian's concern. The doorknob jiggled, and when it refused to open, I slapped the glass surface. "Come on, open. Damn it."

I crumpled to the floor into an upright curled position, wrapping arms around my knees. Gulping in deep breaths did not stop the crying.

"Holly?" Christian's soft baritone filled my ear. "What's wrong?"

I continued to hide my face—forehead planted firmly on my knees. He can't see me like this.

I had nothing left. No children, no husband, and no mother... what is there to live for?

Emptiness flooded into my heart. Tightness clutched at my chest, threatening to suffocate me.

One by one, I lost friends over the years because of infertility grief. I guess I pushed them away. They never knew I cried at home after hearing pregnancy announcements or attending baby showers. They didn't understand how deep their sympathetic words of, 'It'll happen in God's time,' cut. What did they know? Praying brought me nothing.

They also never understood why Deacon and I didn't adopt a baby. Either they didn't care or never even tried, no matter how many times I explained it. No one comprehended it. I just wanted to be like them. To have that reminder of what my body couldn't do. I couldn't do it. I wasn't ready to adopt.

Sobs tore through me, wracking my body in waves. I gasped between tears but couldn't catch my breath. My dream of having a family... dead.

A warm hand rubbed slow circular motions across my upper back, taming back my dark sorrows. The simple gesture deflated my sense of loneliness.

"You go ahead and cry."

The sobs came harder. Mom used to say the same thing.

When all my friends abandoned me, my mother became my best friend. Then she died. Deacon was there through it, but we never connected on a personal level. In the months after Mom's death, talking to one another dwindled to nonexistent. I drove him away just like I drove away my friends. It's my fault... all of it.

"You've come to the right place. In here, we're all fighting a war inside us. It's nice to see you are too," Christian murmured.

A choked laugh escaped from my tight throat. I pulled down my shirt sleeves and mopped my wet face. His eyes watched. "Wanna talk about it?"

I shook my head.

Christian pulled me from the floor. "Come with me. I know just the cure."

"Where are we going?"

His lips twitched. The half-grin made its appearance again. The scars on his face must have something to do with that. "I'll give ya a hint. It's green."

I shrugged. "I dunno."

"Well, you're no fun. You could have at least tried to guess," he teased. "You and I are gonna go get the shelter's Christmas tree."

"I don't feel like it."

Christian slipped his hand inside mine and tugged. "Come on. I know the best place in town."

"Didn't you hear me? I said, no."

"Nope, not taking no for an answer. Now, you comin' or do I need to force you?"

"Why do you care?"

"Lemme tell ya somethin'. In here we support one another. So, what'll it be?" Those blue eyes softened.

"Fine," I sighed. "But no Christmas music."

FIVE

Christian slammed the door shut on his 1970s Ford pickup. He tossed aside a plastic bag and blew into his hands, rubbing them together. "B-r-r-r... it's freezing out there."

"What did you buy?" The plastic crinkled as I separated the stuck edges. Inside were half a dozen packages of candy orange slices. I laughed. "I was right."

"On what?" Christian shifted the truck into reverse and backed up in the convenience store parking lot.

"That you eat candy orange slices. You tasted like it yesterday when we kissed." I tore open the package and plopped a candy in my mouth.

Christian shrugged. "It's a better addiction than pain meds."

"You were a druggie?"

"A long time ago. Noel helped me get clean and offered me a job at the shelter for a room and food."

"What are you? I mean, I know you work in the infirmary, but how much medical training have you had?"

"Former Army Doctor." Christian gripped the steering wheel, never taking his eyes off the red traffic light. "Am I taking you to the Saint Aurora's hospital?"

"Yeah. You turn right at the next street and it's about halfway down the block."

The light switched to green, and the truck's exhaust roared. I swallowed the last piece of candy right as the hospital came into view. "You can park in the patients' lot."

Christian said nothing but complied. He eased the pickup into the parking lot and parked in the closest space to the entrance. His hands stayed on the steering wheel.

I lifted the door handle, unable to complete opening the door. What Christian must have dealt with overseas… while I get uncomfortable seeing a burn victim. It's time to get out of the obstetrics ward and push myself.

"You gettin' out or what?" he asked.

I opened my mouth, but no words came out. His scars solidified my need to get out of my comfort zone.

Christian touched the scars on his face. "Does it bother you that much?"

"What happened?"

"IED shrapnel." He dragged a fingertip across them, showing no signs of feeling it.

"I changed my mind. I'd like to work with you in the infirmary."

Shaking his head, Christian gave a half-smile. He shifted the pickup into gear and drove out of the lot. "I hope you know what you're up against. Every nurse I've had quit."

"Did you kiss them too?"

"Only you. It was an exception."

It was difficult to decide if he was jesting or if he meant it. For a man who appeared to be in his early forties, Christian probably had kissed lots of women. The thought perturbed me. It shouldn't, except I wanted to kiss him again. The back of my neck tingled from yesterday's memory.

"You're still thinking about that kiss, aren't you?" Christian asked.

"What? No…"

Christian chortled.

I gazed out the window, avoiding the smug look I'm sure he had. Don't forget what Deacon did to you. I was thankful Christian didn't add anything more, and that he turned on the radio.

After battling congested traffic for two hours, we drove through the rich section of Saint Aurora. I admired the houses, each decorated to their style. Deacon and I could never afford a house because of the steep costs of fertility procedures. It wasn't fair. My life plans fell apart.

Christian stopped in the driveway of a house that had a wreath hanging on its front door.

All that money wasted on infertility treatments. I ogled at the beautiful gray house. Clear Christmas lights, intertwined with pine garland, were wrapped around the porch railing. The house belonged with the ones shown on TV.

"You comin'? We've got decorations to haul out to the truck," said Christian.

"Where are we?"

Christian gave that stupid half-grin. "Come with me and find out."

"I'll stay here."

His bright blue eyes mimicked the puppy dog look. "Please?"

"No."

The driver's door shut, and he jogged around the front of the pickup to my side. My door flew open. A snowfall began, like someone had shaken a snow globe. It swirled, sticking to everything. Christian's charcoal beanie exchanged its color for white. He tipped his head toward the sky and laughed when the snowflakes caught in his long, black eyelashes.

Mom did that the last time we ice skated. The childish antics made my lips curve into a smile. She always told me I was too serious.

"C'mon." Christian grabbed my hand and pulled me from the truck. He twirled me, never letting go.

We danced in the winter wonderland. When I stumbled, Christian caught me, and I gasped. Our eyes connected with one another.

My mouth dried. Despite his scars, he was the first man I could not deny an attraction for. Deacon. Don't forget about Deacon. "We better go."

Christian agreed.

Our footsteps smeared the fresh snow blanket on the sidewalk leading to the house. On the porch, we stomped the snow off our feet.

A woman dressed in a maid's outfit answered the door. "You must be from the shelter, come on in."

Inside, a gingerbread aroma lingered in the air. I took a deep breath and inhaled its spiciness. Mom and I had spent our Christmas Eves baking and decorating gingerbread men. A lump formed in my throat. I had no one to share this tradition with anymore.

Christian and the woman talked about the shelter.

Someone played "Away in a Manger" on the piano, stopping at a sour note. A female voice encouraged the player to start again. It must be a child receiving a piano lesson. I envied them. My mom couldn't afford piano lessons for me.

I meandered past the foyer, stopping at the edge of a sitting room. Through the archway a girl and woman sat together at a baby grand piano. The melody began again.

A hand on my shoulder startled me. "I need your help to carry those boxes out," Christian whispered. He nudged me toward the foyer.

On our third and final trip of hauling boxes, Christian received what looked like a check from the maid. He stuffed it in his coat pocket. "I'll give it to him."

As we walked back to the pickup, I asked, "What did she give you?"

"Money for her brother." Christian set his box in the truck bed and took mine.

I wanted him to say more, but he didn't.

The engine rumbled to life. Christian cleared the snow off the windshield, using the wipers. "Noel will be glad for the new decorations."

We left the neighborhood in silence. Later, Christian twisted the radio knob and "Silent Night" blared out its chorus. He sang along.

Will the daily reminders that Mom is dead ever stop? I clicked off the radio.

"Don't like Christmas music?"

I hid the tears wetting my blinking eyes. "Not right now."

"I could go for a hot chocolate. How 'bout you?"

I didn't reply.

Christian went through a coffee café's drive-thru and ordered two hot chocolates. He paid and said something like thanks to the cashier.

I sniffled.

"Try it." Christian extended the cup. "It's the best place in the city for hot chocolate."

"Thanks." I snapped off the lid. My mouth watered at the whipped cream and drizzled chocolate floating on top.

Christian leaned forward and opened the glove compartment. He removed two peppermint sticks. "Do you want a peppermint stick to stir with?"

"Please."

Our fingers brushed together. I held onto the peppermint stick longer than needed. "Th… thanks," I mumbled.

"Anytime."

Only the truck's engine talked on the drive back to the shelter. Christian's presence provided the comfort I sought yet allowed me to be alone with my thoughts. I missed my mom.

At the shelter Noel directed a group of men stringing Christmas lights on the front entrance. He smiled and waved as we parked in the circular driveway.

Christian opened the door. "What's this? You started without me."

Noel laughed. It hadn't changed its effect on me. The man had to be Santa Claus. Noel wore a Santa hat and red jacket that highlighted his trimmed white beard. If he wasn't… well, he just has to be.

I observed Noel and Christian while they talked. They exhibited a familiarity with one another that they didn't share with the others at the shelter. It had to be a father-son relationship, or they were close friends.

Christian headed for the truck.

I got out. "Where do you want the boxes?"

"Noel said to leave them by his desk, and they'll go through them after finishing here."

I grunted upon lifting a box that was heavier than I expected. The box slipped, and I staggered. I readjusted my hold.

"Do you want me to take that?" asked Christian.

"No, I got it," I said through gritted teeth.

Christian raised his hands. "Okay."

I turned toward the building. The heavy box threw off my balance, and hands rescued me from hitting the pavement. I gasped. "Th… thanks."

The box lay on the ground with its contents scattered. Christian did not let me go. "It's okay to ask for help. We all need it from time to time."

My body trembled. "Not me," I whispered.

"You've been alone too long."

"Please. I have nothing left to give." I wriggled out of his arms and sprinted inside the shelter. Everyone I cared about eventually left. He would, too.

Six

I examined the cozy infirmary Christian had given a tour of. It was enough to help the homeless veterans with minor issues. Somehow, it felt lacking compared to what I had visualized. "This is it?"

"Yup." Christian opened the door, and a man stood just outside it with a hand applying pressure on his forearm. He directed the patient to the exam table. "Move your hand, so I can see if you need stitches."

"Think I need at least a couple."

"I'd say about three or four." Christian went to the cupboard.

"Excuse me, ma'am." A burly man stood in the infirmary's doorway, wringing a worn baseball cap. "Someone said I could get aspirin here."

I gestured at the empty chair. "You can take a seat here."

"Holly, can you find the gauze please?" Christian asked. He opened a suture kit and prepared for suturing.

"Purdy name."

"I'll uh… be right with you." I gave an awkward giggle.

"Now, please," said Christian.

"Right. Um… the gauze." I turned around and glanced over my shoulder. The man's southern drawl intrigued me regarding how he came to be in Minnesota. His accent made me want to listen to him talk for the sake of talking.

"The gauze is in the upper farthest right cabinet with the bandages."

I found the gauze where Christian said it was. It surprised me to see how well he organized the infirmary's meager medical supplies. The stranger's eyes followed me as I walked toward Christian. I snuck a glimpse and stumbled.

The metal tray with the suture supplies clattered against the floor. Christian steadied me. "Are you alright?"

"Yeah," I mumbled, my cheeks growing warm.

Christian took the gauze. His lips twitched like he wanted to say something, but he didn't. He redirected his attention back to his patient.

I kneeled and gathered the supplies and tray.

A hand held out a pair of scissors. "You missed one."

"Thanks."

"Jared Corbin."

"What can I do for you, Jared Corbin?"

"Aspirin, please."

"For what?" I placed the dirtied items beside the sink and pumped soap into my palm. It lathered under the running water. I scrubbed in-between my fingers, further lathering the soap.

"Headache."

"Do you have headaches often?"

Jared stepped in close, almost touching me. Stale smoke mingled with Old Spice aftershave radiated off him. "Occasionally. Aspirin does the trick."

"Christian should look at you." I let the water drip off my hands.

"Will you go for a walk with me?" Jared secured his cap on his head. His amber-colored eyes crinkled when he smiled. They were like Deacon's in our earlier years.

"I-I-I—"

"Please? Give a guy hope?" His dark, long eyelashes fluttered with each blink.

"Su—"

"She's busy," said Christian, resting a hand on my shoulder.

Jared's posture drooped. "Oh, maybe I'll see you around."

"Here's your aspirin, take 'em and leave." Christian shoved the packet against Jared's chest. They engaged in a short staring contest.

"Okay, okay, okay, I'm leavin'."

After Jared left, my hands rushed to my hips, and I glared at Christian. "Jealous, are we?"

"I don't trust the guy. Stay away from him."

"I'm a thirty-five-year-old woman, and I certainly don't need you to tell me who I can and can't associate with."

Christian sighed. "Holly…"

"Hey, Doc," said Chloe, standing in the doorway gazing at us. "Uh, is this a bad time?"

"No, we're finished talking," I replied.

I fumed over everything about Christian. The man insisted on escorting me everywhere for my safety, which annoyed me. Noel would never allow violent people in the shelter. Would he?

That stupid kiss would not leave my mind. What kind of man kisses women for no reason? Stop it, it was just a kiss. And it woke something up inside you, something that had died a long time ago.

I growled. A peaceful courtyard outside my dorm window beckoned my name. Perhaps the fresh air would help take my mind off the infuriating Christian.

Dusk drifted below the horizon by the time I located the courtyard, but I didn't care. I found freedom for the first time since my arrival at the shelter. I pushed open the door.

The brisk winter air attacked, and I gasped at its coldness. I continued into the courtyard. A brief walk revealed a bench that had been cleared of snow. I sat on it, admiring the sunset. Pink and orange hues sunk farther in the sky, and the moon made its milky-white appearance. The outside lights turned on one by one, finishing with a pine tree.

A shadow limped into the dim lights until a man's face came into view. "What are you doing out here?" he asked.

I glanced at the man's baby face. It was hard to imagine him as a soldier on the battlefield, much less a grown man. "How did I get here? How does anybody end up here?"

"You're as pretty as they say you are." The man seated himself beside me and held out a hand. "Name's Dylan Thornton."

"Holly Bradford."

His brown eyes peered into mine. "After my last tour, I came home to find that my wife took our two sons and left. Later she filed for divorce and full-time custody. I can't work because I'm in too much pain with my back and knees, but I can't afford myself because child support takes most of my paycheck, leaving me with two hundred dollars to live on."

I nibbled my bottom lip, unsure how to respond to his plight

"I know, poor me."

"My husband disappeared without a trace and left divorce papers, and I'm not sure how I should feel." I whispered.

"That's tough. How long were you married?"

"Twelve years. I have to confess it became like we were roommates."

"Like a security blanket, right?"

I shrugged. He didn't need to know about my infertility woes, and how I had driven away Deacon. "I guess."

"You've suffered more loss than that, haven't you?"

"Dylan…" I let out a long exhale. "I don't want to talk about it."

"Me either. It's why my wife divorced me because I couldn't talk to her about what happened overseas."

"Holly." Christian's baritone voice clipped. He stepped into the light and scowled at Dylan. "Why didn't you tell me you wanted to go to the courtyard?"

"Did it ever occur to you I'm tired of you being around all the time," I snapped. "Why is it I'm the only one that needs an escort on the grounds?" I stomped off without waiting for a reply.

Christian called me.

I kept going. Who did he think he was?

A pair of boot steps crunched behind. "Holly, what is going on with you? Tell me please," Christian implored.

"Why do you care?"

"Because I like you."

I stopped. "What?"

"Um, uh I—"

"I can't do this," I said, ignoring my heart's quickening pitter-patter.

Christian inched forward. "He hurt you, didn't he?"

"Yes… No… I'm not sure…"

"What did he do, cheat on you?"

I stiffened. "Christian, I can't."

"Why?" asked Christian, interlacing his fingers in mine.

I slapped them and whirled around toward the door.

"Tell me, why can't you?"

"Because I'm still married."

Silence.

I marched inside the shelter and didn't look back. It was time to face Deacon and his packet's contents.

My fingers rattled against the doorknob to my room. I could do this. I had to do this. The door creaked open. I clenched my jaw and forged forward where the package lay in wait.

Like I had suspected, divorce papers were inside. Deacon had already signed them and marked where my signature was required. I rummaged in my purse for a pen.

My pen hovered over the signature line. Thirteen years together and married for twelve…

I skimmed through the document, signing where there was a tab. The lump in my throat grew with each page turn, making it difficult to swallow.

… gone in a few signatures.

Deacon left nothing. He had drained our bank accounts and disappeared, all with intentions of leaving me with nothing.

I flipped to the last page and dropped my pen. Deacon had left a note.

> *Dear Holly,*
>
> *I couldn't bear to see the disappointment on your face and decided it would be best to leave a note as we part ways. Divorce is something I have been thinking about for a while. Neither one of us are happy anymore.*
>
> *I apologize for leaving you with nothing, but I've become involved with—*

The paper fluttered to the floor. Noel was right. Deacon was a coward and didn't deserve me.

I thought I would cry after facing what was in the package, but I surprised myself. Was it relief? Or was it numbness? I fixated on the paper I had dropped until it and everything around it became a blur. Who am I?

My identity as Deacon's wife no longer existed. I am me, and only me. There was no separation period where

I could entertain being alone. He had ripped off the scab without warning.

"You okay?" Chloe's voice wove its way into my trance.

I shook my head.

Chloe scooped up the note, setting it on the nightstand with the divorce papers. She yelped. Her arms wrapped around her baby bump. "The little brat is bent on making me miserable."

"You should count yourself lucky. I'd give anything to even experience that," I snapped. My hands covered my mouth. "I'm... so sorry."

Chloe gaped.

I waited for her to run out.

Instead, she slumped on the bed. "You can't have kids?"

I stared at the wall, wanting to avoid the pity look I had seen all too often from others. "The doctors don't know why."

"Why didn't you adopt?"

"I was too ashamed," I whispered.

"Why? Adopting a child doesn't mean you're a failure."

Tension built up behind my eyes. I blinked. "It doesn't matter anymore, my husband... er... ex-husband now — left me with nothing. No money. No home."

"When I got shipped stateside, I ran away."

"Why? Where are your parents?"

"I'm AWOL." She faced me. "Please don't say anything, I'll get arrested. I can't go back."

I motioned a zipper across my lips. "What will you do when the baby is born?"

"Give it up for adoption. After that, I don't know."

"You can't think you'll run for the rest of your life?"

Chloe rose. "You don't get it. I'm the one that will be punished while nothing happens to him."

"How do you know unless you turn him in for what he did to you?"

"Forget I told you anything." Chloe stormed out of my room.

I messed up. I shouldn't have pushed her. She wasn't ready. I had forgotten my training on how to deal with sexual assault victims. Because of my screw-up, I might have set her back.

Chloe's 'nothing will happen to him' statement rang in my ears. It related to me. I brushed my fingers across the divorce papers.

I stuffed them in the envelope without reading through it again. It was time to bring them to the courthouse. I glanced at my wristwatch. It was a quarter after six. Filing the divorce papers would have to wait until tomorrow morning.

SEVEN

My roommate whimpered and rolled onto her side in a fetal position. I squinted at the alarm clock's dim glow and sighed. Four hours remained until the courthouse opened. The metal clasp on the packet glinted.

I sat upright in bed and brought it closer. Its contents would change my life forever once the courthouse filed it. Another one of my failures. I couldn't have kids, and now, I couldn't hold our marriage together. The envelope flap creased under my fingertips.

In the faint light, I traced Deacon's handwriting across the front. His scrawl broke off after my name, like our marriage. Along the way, in wanting a baby, I had forgotten to want him for him. No wonder we had become strangers.

I set the package back on the nightstand and lay down in bed with my fingers interlaced behind my head. The ceiling offered nothing to count. One sheep. Two sheep. My mind continued churning thoughts. I shifted to my side and faced the wall.

Sleep continued to elude me despite laying there for what seemed like hours. I tossed back the covers. Someone had created a coffee perfume that proved irresistible in my restless state. I grabbed my bathrobe and tiptoed out the door.

Hushed voices came from the lounge.

When I entered, Christian and Chloe stopped talking and glanced at me. "Morning," I mumbled, pouring a cup of coffee.

Christian averted his gaze. "Chloe and I are going on a run. Would you like to join?"

"No, thanks." I tied my gaping robe shut.

Christian said to Chloe, "I'll meetcha at the elevator."

She nodded and left the room.

Christian's blue eyes bored into mine. The silence stretched to a long minute until he spoke. "Can we talk about yesterday?"

"Christian…"

"If you don't want me to escort you anymore, then fine. Things happen here that you don't understand because you aren't military." Christian paused by my side and took my hand. His stare never wavered. "I don't want you hurt."

A tingle started where he caressed. "Please don't."

"I would never hurt you."

"I can't." I freed my hand from his.

"Noel told me. Why didn't you tell me?"

"It doesn't matter anymore. I'm going to the courthouse this morning and filing the divorce papers he left behind." I shrugged.

"Want me to take you?"

"I'll ask Noel."

"Why? I said I'd go with you."

"So, um… why are you running with Chloe?"

"Really? Is this how it's going to be, Holly?" Christian scuffed the toe of his shoe on the floor and glanced at the door. "I have to go. Chloe's waiting for me."

"Wait…" I touched his arm, but he pulled it out of reach.

"I am not your husband, so don't treat me like I'm him." Christian stormed out of the lounge.

I twirled my wedding ring, loosening it off the finger where it had resided for so long that a permanent indentation remained there. The simple ring held little meaning now. I held it up and examined the single diamond that had dulled because of lack of care.

"Are you sure you're ready to do this?" asked Noel.

I shoved the ring in my coat pocket. "In a few more minutes."

An empty candy bag lay on the center bench seat. Had I known Noel borrowed Christian's pickup, I would have found another means of transportation. Yet the empty bag brought me solace. Perhaps I had been too hasty in declining Christian's offer to go with me.

Over the faded hood, I observed people proceeding through the courthouse's revolving doors. I clutched at the packet that would change my future. "How did you know about Deacon leaving me?"

"Christmas magic." Noel winked.

Tears formed in my eyes, and a lump began in my throat. "I'm not sure I believe in it anymore."

"I think Santa has a special present for you this year." Noel hugged me. A sugar cookie odor permeated his jacket, like he had been baking cut-out cookies.

His words renewed my tears. "I think both him and God forgot about me," I whispered.

"You need to let it go."

"Let what go?"

"What your life should have looked like."

"I do not hold onto what my life should have been."

"You're like your mother, Holly," said Noel, tucking a stray hair behind my ear.

"How—"

A knock at the window sounded. I cranked the window down a crack.

"Are you folks planning to go in?" asked a uniformed security guard. "You've been sitting here for thirty minutes, and, if you aren't, you need to move along."

I moistened my lips and held up the package. "I uh… was mentally preparing myself. Divorce papers."

"Would you like me to escort you to the Clerk's office?"

"I'll take her," said Noel. He opened his door. "Third floor, right?"

The guard nodded. "Been here before?"

"You could say that. Holly, are you ready?"

It had been four days since Deacon's disappearance and no word from the police. Dead or alive, Deacon had left me with nothing. We were over. I clenched my jaw and pressed the envelope against my chest. "Let's get this over with."

We walked through the parking lot in silence. The closer we approached the courthouse entrance, the faster my insides jiggled. I can't believe this is happening. We could have worked this out, I… I…

The packet fell to the sidewalk. I yanked off my mittens and struggled with grasping the package.

Noel placed his hand on my arm. "You'll get past this."

"I don't know what happened." Liar.

"I got divorced once." Noel picked up the envelope and gave it back to me. "Come, let's go inside and I'll tell you more." He nudged me toward the courthouse lobby.

After the security guards had us walk through the metal detector, Noel and I collected our items in a tote at the end of the conveyor belt. We joined a small crowd waiting for the elevator.

"Why did you get a divorce?" I asked.

"I was young and too foolish to understand what a marriage meant. Getting married is the simple part, it's the holding it together that is difficult because no one ever breathes a word on how hard it is to compromise."

"She left you?"

"We wanted different things and I wouldn't compromise with her until it was too late. By then, I had broken her heart."

The elevator dinged. Noel ushered me inside and pressed the button for the third floor.

"You try getting her back?"

"Three years passed before I tracked her down. She wouldn't return phone calls and sent back my letters, so one day I waited outside her apartment."

"And?"

Noel smiled. "I saw her walking down the street with a little girl holding onto her hand. They sat on the front steps, eating their ice cream cones and laughing. She seemed so happy that I left without talking to her."

"She moved on—"

"This is our floor." Noel gestured at the opened elevator doors. We weaved through the full elevator and stepped into the hallway. He pointed at a doorway. "The clerk's office is at the end."

"Will you come in with me?"

"Holly… you will find happiness again. It may not seem like it, but Deacon will regret his decision."

"I doubt it," I muttered.

"Stop blaming yourself."

"Why? If we would have had kids, he would have stayed."

"He is an addict. You know having kids wouldn't have changed anything," said Noel.

"I don't want to talk about this anymore." I walked past him and into the clerk's office.

Eight

Noel's office seemed to have shrunk with both of us at his desk. Somehow, it had seemed bigger before. People talking in the lobby made it difficult to concentrate on what he was teaching.

Noel pointed at the computer screen. "Once you type in their name, you snap a picture of them with the webcam."

"Why do you enter all this information about them?"

"The more information we compile about them, the more we're able to help them." Noel removed a stack of photos and letters from a drawer and laid them on the desk. "All these are past guests."

I caressed a wedding photograph of a beautiful couple, underneath was a brief thank you note. "You heal what is broken," I murmured.

"Pete," said Noel.

The male deputy stood in the doorway, fidgeting with his gloves. "I need to speak with Holly."

Noel excused himself.

I opened the drawer he had removed the stack from. On top was a faded picture of my mother and me around ten years old.

Pete stepped forward. "I looked into your husband—"

"Ex." I slammed the drawer shut.

"What?"

"Deacon is my ex-husband. I signed the divorce papers he left behind, the only thing he bothered to leave behind other than questions."

Pete laid his gloves on the empty chair. "I learned he was a heavy gambler and that he probably feared for his life. Deacon owed a lot of money."

"Explains why he drained our bank account, but I knew that. He told me in his note that he slipped in the divorce papers."

"Did he tell you anything about a crime?"

"A crime?" Deacon listened to his clients, who confided in him about the crimes they had committed. He would never get involved with one of them. I shook my head. "He's a lawyer. His only crime is helping criminals get off."

"He may have witnessed a murder. On December first, somebody reported a dead body, and when we traced the call, it led to Deacon."

"Wh… where is he?"

"That's the weird part. It's like he disappeared. There's no trail to follow where Deacon may have gone, or if the murderers have him."

"What does that mean?"

"I think he's hiding in town somewhere." Pete scuffed the floor with the toe of his boot and stared at the black mark he had left behind.

"Am I in danger?"

He locked his eyes on mine. "The shelter is the safest place to be. They'd have to be fools to go after you in a building full of veterans."

"I was home that night…" A slow burn started in my throat. That evening had served as a cruel reminder of my failure. "Deacon left after eight-thirty. Something at his work came up, but I don't know what to believe anymore." I sighed.

"You'll get through this." Pete lifted his gloves and twisted them around his fingers. A woman's voice garbled a slew of words over his radio unit. He pressed the button, responding in police jargon.

Beyond the opened door, Noel stood talking to a man with a large green duffle bag slung over his shoulder.

Jared hovered right outside Noel's office. He grinned and waved at me while I thanked Pete for his help.

Pete scribbled something on a business card and laid it on the desk. "This is my personal cellphone number. Call me if you need anything. Walk me out?"

"Sure, just a second." I paused where Jared stood. "I'll be with you in a few moments."

"Meet me outside? I need a smoke," said Jared.

"I'll try."

Jared went ahead, passing by Noel and the man as he exited the building.

Pete and I lingered in the lobby and exchanged last minute words. Throughout our conversation, Noel's companion stared at Pete. When Pete turned, the man shouted, "Gun! Get down!"

Renewed echoes reiterated the words in a continuous stream. The man lunged at Pete, tackling him down to the floor. His fists jabbed at various spots on Pete's body.

The shelter's security guards pried the two men apart.

Super soldier fended them off and leaped at Pete again. "I won't let you kill my men!"

Someone's screams added to the shouts' din. I covered my mouth, and they stopped.

Pete crisscrossed his arms across his face, protecting himself against the stranger's knuckles.

A security guard grabbed the irate man around the waist and pulled him off.

"Let me go," the soldier growled.

Pete scrambled, removing something from his belt just as his attacker knocked out his capturer. The contraption in his hands spit out wires at the sprinting man.

The veteran jolted, crumbling to the floor. His body twitched, like he was having an epileptic seizure.

"Get Christian," Noel ordered someone. His voice broke my stunned state of staring at the restrained attacker.

I blinked. Was he talking to me?

"Wh... wh... why?" The man quivered.

Noel squatted beside the veteran and touched his shoulder. He said in a gentle tone, "You're safe here. No one is here to hurt you."

"Damn," Pete muttered, checking on the unconscious security guard. He radioed for an ambulance. "Who is this guy?"

"Holly, are you okay? You're shaking," said Noel.

I raised my hands and found I was. I took a deep breath and exhaled slowly. "What happened?"

"He—"

"The reason you need an escort with you," Christian interjected. He kneeled beside the groaning security guard and moved a finger back and forth in front of his eyes. "The ambulance is on the way. You need to get that concussion checked out farther."

"Do I have to?" The guard rubbed his head.

"It's being on the safe side." Christian tilted his head toward the belligerent veteran. "Get him up to the infirmary. I'll be there in a minute."

"You're back. I thought," I sputtered.

"I was at the treatment center helping Leila."

"Why?"

"Are you comin' with me to the infirmary or not?" Icy blue eyes narrowed. "Ya know what, forget it."

I chased after him, apologizing.

Christian stopped after the first flight of stairs. "My patient is waiting."

"You were right."

"Come on, time to learn about PTSD."

We continued to the infirmary, where the veteran rocked himself on the exam table. He whimpered multiple times.

"Talk to him," whispered Christian.

I mouthed, "No."

Christian threw up his hands. He tiptoed forward. "I'm Doctor Christian Hunt. What's your name?"

"PFC Eric Hardbeck."

"What's that mean?" I asked.

"Private First Class," Christian replied. "I need to take your vitals. Can you please remove your jacket?"

"No!" exclaimed Eric.

"You got shocked by a taser. It's my duty to make sure you're okay."

Eric tugged his jacket closer to his body. "You're not touching me."

"Did someone hurt you?" I asked.

"Not talkin' about that."

I eased the vitals machine beside him. "Where did you grow up? I've lived in Saint Aurora my whole life."

"New York City."

"Why don't you tell me about it?"

"My grandma raised my little brother and me…" As Eric continued talking, he loosened his grip.

I removed his jacket without protest and secured the blood pressure cuff around his arm. "You will feel some pressure on your arm."

Eric grunted but didn't flinch. The cuff pumped full of air then deflated at a slow pace, beeping the results.

"Your systolic pressure is a little low."

"That's expected," said Christian. "Eric, have you thought about getting treatment for PTSD? I can call and get you in a treatment center."

"I'm not going back there."

"Does your little brother know you're here?" I unfastened the cuff off Eric's arm and tucked it back into its basket.

"He's dead."

"I'm sorry for your loss. When?"

"Month ago." Eric shifted his shirt collar. "Can I still stay here? I'm awful sorry about my behavior."

"If Noel allows it, you will be required to talk to someone." Christian folded his arms across his chest.

"How about her?"

"Absolutely not, Holly doesn't have any experience with what you've dealt with in the military."

"Can I talk to you in the hallway?" I glared at Christian.

"This is not up for discussion. Eric will either have sessions with me or another medical professional."

"But—"

"Do I make myself clear?"

I mumbled an agreement. "If you're finished with my services, I need to get back to Noel."

Jared met me in the hallway. "Noel told me you was here. Are ya okay?"

"I'm fine. What did you need?"

"Wanted to see ya again."

"I don't have time right now." I started for the elevator. "Maybe later?"

"How 'bout breakfast?"

"Yeah, fine. Tomorrow." The elevator dinged, and I got on alone.

NINE

A bright red stain inside my underwear taunted me. A sinking feeling settled into my heart at Mother Nature's cruel reminder of another failure. "Damn it." I slammed my palm against the metal bathroom stall. With everything going on, I had to deal with a period too.

Someone turned on the water at the sink.

"Can you please get me a tampon?" I asked.

The woman didn't respond.

I wrapped toilet paper around my hand, prepared to line my underwear. A tampon appeared under the stall door. I took it and mumbled, "Thanks."

The woman still said nothing.

I flushed the toilet and opened the stall door.

Chloe stood in front of the sink. Her eyes remained unblinking as she stared into the mirror. She never acknowledged my presence.

"You're a lifesaver." I pumped the soap.

Chloe's breaths came in short spurts. She tightened her grip on the sink's edge, her knuckles blanching.

"Chloe, what's wrong?" I placed a hand on her arm.

She lurched. "Don't touch me!"

"You were reliving when you learned you were pregnant, weren't you?"

Her hands shook. She inhaled sharply. "I was on tour in Afghanistan."

"Did you tell anyone what happened?"

Chloe hardened her face. "Who would believe a private, especially one on her first tour?"

"Report him anyway."

"You don't get it. I can't."

"Who was it, Chloe? Tell me."

"My—"

The women's bathroom door swung open and someone entered. An opportunity escaped for learning more about her rapist. Chloe bolted past the intruder.

"Chloe." I darted after her.

She stopped in the hallway and spoke with her back facing me. "Go away and leave me alone."

"I just want to help you."

"Don't you get it? There is no helping me," Chloe snapped. She advanced farther down the hallway and into her room. The door slammed.

I wanted to understand. She seemed afraid to report the man who raped her. Justice in the military couldn't be that different than regular justice. I combed my fingers through my long ponytail. That's why Christian ran with Chloe in the mornings. He knew. How dare he not report her plight.

If he wouldn't, then I would. I marched down the hallway and found Christian lounging outside the elevator.

"I wondered if you were ever coming," he said.

"Did you know?"

"Know what?"

I jabbed him in the chest. "About Chloe's situation?"

"Whatever you're thinkin', don't."

"It needs to be reported." I tapped the elevator's down button.

When it arrived, Christian blocked the opened doors. "It needs to be her decision, not yours."

"I don't understand. Why are you against this?"

"Because you solve everyone's problems instead of your own. I saw it with Dylan, and I saw with Eric yesterday."

"Get out of my way."

"You need to sort through your own issues. Talk to me. Talk to Noel. Talk to somebody, but quit interfering with other people's troubles." Christian removed his hand.

I entered the elevator. "What do you know about my problems," I muttered, banging the lobby button several times. At least I never turned to drugs like he did.

"Holly…" Christian sighed. He leapt inside before the doors shut. "Underneath that caregiver exterior of yours, I see the grief and I see the anger. I only recognize it because I've been there, maybe it's not the same as yours, but I still felt it. If you don't resolve it, it'll consume you."

When the elevator reached the ground floor, I pushed past him and into the lobby.

Christian hollered after me, "I'm telling you this because I care."

Noel was not in his office. I slumped into the chair and used the office phone. The line rang half a dozen times. "Hello, this is Pete," he answered.

Christian's words replayed in a loop.

"Is anyone there? Noel, are you okay?" asked Pete.

The phone clattered in the cradle. I hunched over, putting my elbows on the desk and covered my mouth with balled up hands. Mom always called this position, my thinking pose.

Christian was right. I focused on other people's problems, so I had little time to work on my own. My stomach churned.

It had to do with control. I controlled nothing in my life, and by helping others, it was a way of maintaining some. If I couldn't give myself happiness, at least I provided happiness to others.

The phone's ring startled me. "Reed Shelter, this is Holly."

"Did someone call from there?" asked Pete.

"It was me. I thought I needed your help but changed my mind. I'm sorry."

"If you need me, don't be afraid to call. Talk to you later."

Noel appeared in the doorway the same time I hung up the phone. He winked. "Taking over my office already?"

My eyes grew dewy. I faked a small smile and nodded.

Noel stepped aside. "Holly?"

I sniffled. "What?"

"I'm here if you need a listening ear."

"Thanks. I'll see you later." I ambled toward the lobby.

Christian still lingered around the elevator, like he had been waiting for me. "I'm sorry, Holly. I shouldn't have said that."

"You were right."

Christian clasped my hand and caressed it. "Can I get that in writing?" he teased.

A tingle started at my nape. It'd been a long time since a man touched me like that. No, as much as I enjoyed it, Deacon's betrayal remained too fresh. "Don't."

Christian did not follow me onto the elevator. For that I was grateful. As the steel doors closed, my reflection glared back. My outside appearance screamed a put-together person but was far from the truth. I had lied to myself all these years.

I hated confrontations and avoided them. Was that why I lied to myself? Was that why I still clung to the hope Deacon would come back, and our comfortable life would resume? Do I love Deacon?

The elevator stopped and Dylan limped on. "Hi, how are you?"

"Confused." The word tumbled out of my mouth. I tucked my tongue between my teeth.

Dylan's brown eyes met mine. "The past, huh?"

"How did you know?"

"After my ex-wife left, I struggled moving forward. A person prefers to stick with what's familiar, which in your case was your husband. It's hard work learning what you're capable of alone."

"I filed the divorce papers a few days ago."

Dylan nodded. "How do you feel?"

"I don't know."

"Yes, you do. You don't want to admit it because you're afraid people will judge."

"I don't know how. I've lied to myself and everyone all these years…"

The elevator doors opened and there stood Christian talking with Noel. "Start with him." Dylan hobbled into the lobby.

I swallowed. He was right. I hated exposing my flaws. Deacon was the last person I had allowed that privilege, and he left me. Here, at the shelter, everyone shared their flaws. It was a foreign concept, but Dylan was right. I needed to start with Christian.

"You back again? Did you miss me?" Christian jested with a half-smirk.

"Can I talk—"

"Holly," Jared drawled, "ya ready for breakfast?"

Christian stiffened. "You have breakfast plans with *him*?"

I sighed. Jared seemed to come at the most inopportune times. "I forgot we made plans. Can you and I talk later?"

"If you don't forget," Christian mocked.

His response stung. I wanted to see what made Christian skeptical about Jared. Christian's blue eyes pierced through me as I walked away from him. He said nothing more.

TEN

Please, don't do this. These women need you," said Noel into the phone receiver. He glanced and held up a pointer finger in midair. Whoever spoke on the other end must have given an unwanted response, for Noel sighed. "We'll make do without you I suppose…"

He placed the phone in its cradle with a rattle. "Sorry about the delay. How can I help you?"

"I'm leaving as soon as I secure a job and an apartment."

A desk drawer slid open, and Noel removed a white envelope that had my name written on it. "This is for you."

"What is it?"

"Open it." Noel smiled.

I slit the sealed envelope flap and gawked. Bills lined the inside. "How?"

"I worked it out so you can get paid."

"Wow, um, I don't know what to say."

"Say that you'll stay."

I nodded.

"I need your help with something. Come with me."

I folded the envelope in half and jammed it into my jeans pocket. Later today I would open a new bank account, one in my name only. Though I told him I would stay, a part protested.

We ambled down the hallway past the kitchen. "Amy, our volunteer psychologist, informed me she is resigning her post here. Can you run the women's support group until I find a replacement?" Noel paused in front of a shut door.

Through the window, Chloe stood talking to another woman near the refreshments table. I swallowed. She'd walk out if I led the group. How was I supposed to relate to these women? They were veterans and saw combat, unlike me.

"I have faith in you, Holly," said Noel.

"I, um…"

Noel swung open the door and entered. "Afternoon, ladies. I regret to inform you, Amy resigned immediately. Until I find a replacement, Holly will be in charge."

The women stared at me and murmurs rippled through the small group. They hated me already.

I took a deep breath and exhaled it slowly, forcing a smile. "Hello."

"Don't be nervous, you'll do fine," Noel whispered in my ear. He patted my shoulder and left me alone with ten women, survivors of both physical and mental trauma.

Nobody spoke except for the squeak of my chair. I folded my hands in my lap. "Let's do introductions."

Silence.

Crap, this was harder than I thought. I licked my dry lips. "I'm Holly Bradford. Fate brought me here when I met Noel after the hospital let me go."

Clothes rustled. They continued gaping.

"I blew him off at first and went home. The next day I was evicted from my apartment because my husband lied about paying the rent and hid the late notices."

Still no one volunteered to speak.

"Then my husband left a note saying he wanted a divorce. Who does that? Who asks for a divorce through a note after twelve years?"

"Did you at least get money from the divorce?" Chloe asked with widened eyes.

"He withdrew all the money in our joint account to pay for gambling debts." I shook my head. "I had no clue."

A woman put her left leg over her right knee. "What a bastard."

"She's not one of us," said another woman, who frowned and crossed her arms over her chest.

Chloe avoided my gaze.

"I may not have experienced combat, but I will listen," I said.

More stared.

It was no use. They would never accept me. I sighed and rose from my seat when Chloe spoke, "It's true. She is a good listener. I think you should give her a chance."

"How will she help by listening? Amy knew what it was like for us over there." A brown-haired woman glared at Chloe.

Chloe brought her hands to her hips. "Amy is no longer here. Holly is all we've got and if you don't like it, you can leave."

"I may not understand, but I'd like to," I said softly.

The woman's lips twitched, like she couldn't decide on taking a chance on me. "Name's Lisa Gibbons."

"How about you begin today's discussion and I'll listen."

What had started out threatening ended in a good place. Each woman thanked me as they trickled out of the meeting room. I stopped Chloe. "Thanks for sticking up for me."

"I told you, we don't like outsiders." Chloe's lips moved side to side. She lowered her voice, "I'm sorry about the other morning."

Without thinking, I raised my hand. She flinched, and my arm dropped by my side. "Please let me help you."

Chloe turned her head toward the door. "I'll be fine. I have to go."

His arms crossed, Christian had propped himself against the hallway wall along with a boot. "Hey, how'd it go?"

"It was a challenge." I shrugged.

Chloe waddled past and disappeared around the corner.

"She kept the other women from walking out."

"Trust doesn't come easily in here."

"I can't say I blame them. I wasn't in the service and I don't trust easily."

Jared strolled toward Christian and me.

Christian cleared his throat. "Noel asked if we could decorate the Christmas tree in the main lounge. He and the others are starting on the tree in the lobby."

"Hey, Holly, you wannabe my decoratin' partner?" asked Jared.

A lump formed in my throat. Mom and I had always decorated the Christmas tree together, even when she lay in her hospital bed too weak to get up. Deacon never showed interest in helping.

"You're too late. Her and I have been assigned to do the main lounge," said Christian.

Jared rubbed the back of his neck. "Oh, next time, maybe."

When Jared was gone, Christian asked, "Holly?"

"What?

"You comin' with me to decorate?"

"I don't know if I can," I whispered.

"It's your first Christmas, isn't it? That's why you can't listen to Christmas carols."

"My mom loved Christmas."

Christian nodded. "So did my parents. In the town where I grew up, they played Mrs. Claus and Santa Claus."

"Does the pain ever go away?"

"No… but their spirit sticks with ya over the years. When I play Santa Claus, I feel closer to them than any other time of the year."

"You play Santa Claus?"

Christian chuckled. "Every year on Christmas Eve here at the shelter. No one ever plays Mrs. Claus though." He winked.

"We better get that tree decorated for Noel."

Footsteps trailed behind. Christian acknowledged each person who passed by in the hallway.

"Holly, wait."

Someone had hung mistletoe in the lounge's doorway. My heart raced. Christian leaned, and my hands trembled. This was it, the moment I had waited for since he kissed me the first time. To prove I was mistaken about an attraction between us.

His candy orange breath proved tantalizing. I placed my hands on his chest and closed my eyes, waiting for his lips on mine. Instead, his warm breath tickled my cheek. "You're not ready."

Eleven

As the pickup gained speed on the highway, the engine rumbled louder. The radio stayed silent. My fingers ached, deciding whether I should turn it on or leave it off. I folded my hands on my lap. The passing scenery had changed from urban buildings to rural.

Plastic crinkled. Seconds later an orange scent filled the truck cab. Christian must be eating a candy orange slice. I shifted my gaze from the window to him. The scars on his jaw moved in a chewing motion. What had once bothered me, the scars, transformed into a testimonial that he was a survivor.

"Whatcha thinking about?" asked Christian.

I plopped a candy orange slice in my mouth and sucked on it, savoring the citrus flavor. "How your scars reflect more than you surviving war. I know you kicked your drug addiction, what else have you survived?"

Christian tightened his grip on the steering wheel, never responding.

I fiddled with the radio, turning the knob until a clear station tuned in and Christmas music blared. "Turn it down," I shouted, covering my ears.

He twisted a knob beside the one I had used.

"How can you stand listening to loud music?"

Christian shrugged. "Habit."

"Yeah, well… you'll need hearing aids, if you keep that up," I muttered toward the window.

Buildings and traffic became sparse the farther we drove north, and in its place, bare trees and crisp clean snow decorated the landscape. I liked it. The countryside had a soothing way of forcing a person to slow their pace, unlike the city.

I cranked the handle and cracked the window enough for fresh air. Rotting garbage didn't taint the crisp breeze. Pure was the word to describe the country air's smell.

Christian snickered. "Ain't nothing like good ol' country air."

"I've lived in the city my whole life."

"Country boy here."

Christian turned at a sign labeled Hunt's Christmas Tree Farm. The pickup slowed in a long, narrow driveway lined with dense pine trees of all sizes. Snow decorated their boughs. It was what I had imagined a tree farm would look like.

"Where are we?" I asked.

"My family home."

"Your family owns a Christmas tree farm?"

Two men stopped sawing and waved. Christian honked the horn several short times. "Third generation here."

The truck eased to a stop in a gravel driveway. In the forest's heart stood a log cabin style house, and a weathered red barn with large horses outside. A door slammed.

Christian walked around the front of the pickup and opened my door. "I'll give you a tour, starting with our Clydesdales."

I followed him toward the beasts, gasping at their size. The muscular brown and white horses stood taller than any horse I'd ever seen.

He rubbed the horse's snout. "They pull the sleigh."

"Sleigh?" I gaped at them.

"Don't tell me you've never gone on a sleigh ride," Christian teased, pointing at a red contraption parked beside the barn.

I shook my head.

"Wow, you weren't kiddin' when you said you were a city girl. I hope you've at least ice skated."

"Whose house is this?"

The two-story house showed no signs of anyone home. Yet, the owner had decorated the farm, including the barn and the fence. I leaned near the pine garland wrapped around the porch pillars, inhaling the aroma emanating from it.

Christian whispered in my ear, "Mine."

"What? Why are you living at the shelter and not here? It's gorgeous here." I spun around and faced him.

Christian gave my hand a slight tug. "Come on, my surprise is in the backyard."

"Wait, stop."

Christian pulled me along, not answering.

My feet moved underneath me as if they weren't my own. We arrived at a clearing behind the house. I stumbled to a stop.

Christian gestured. "We're here."

The sun rays formed prisms in the ice, causing various color hues to sparkle. Two pairs of ice skates lay on a fallen log near the water's edge. I blinked. "What is this place?"

"I skated here a lot when I was a kid."

"Are you kidding me? I had you pegged more for a hockey player." I looped the skate laces and tied them together.

Christian pulled a hockey stick from behind the log. "You follow hockey?"

I snatched it and skated across the pond, whirling around. My hockey stick banged against the ice as I prepared to launch a snowball. "I lived for hockey in school."

The snowball sailed through the air. "She shoots and she scores!" I raised my arms and spun around near the pond's edge. A cracking noise sped up, and the flat surface underneath jolted.

Screams pierced the air. The thumping of my heart masked real time. My flightless body broke through the ice and jerked at a hard bottom. Something cold and wet slapped my numb face.

Christian raced towards me, his voice distorted.

I gasped, kicking.

Arms grabbed ahold under my armpits and pulled. Christian grunted. Each tug toward the bank threatened to upchuck the contents in my stomach. Christian released a loud groan and heaved me from the last of the water's icy hold. We fell into the snowbank with me landing on top of him.

Christian panted, his blue eyes locking onto mine. "Let's get you inside the house."

My teeth wouldn't stop their chattering. I scooted closer to the fireplace and rubbed my shivering arms and legs. The blanket slipped off my bare shoulders. I covered them and clutched the blanket tighter.

Christian returned with women's clothing. "Here are dry clothes for you."

"Th-th-th...." I settled for a nod.

"My wife and you are about the same size, so the clothes should fit." Christian laid the clothes beside me. His eyes lingered in an upward motion until they met mine. "You scared the hell outta me," he mumbled.

I huddled closer to my knees. A slow burning heat crept past the lump in my throat and escaped through the tears on my cheeks. I jerked at Christian's touch.

"It seems like a lifetime ago since I've lived here."

Christian pressed the gray thermal shirt against his nose. "Her smell is gone." He bunched up the shirt and tossed it, burying his face in his hands. His voice muffled, "I should have known it wouldn't be there after fifteen years."

"Wh-wh-what happened?" I regretted the question the moment my gaze traveled to a curled ultrasound picture leaning on a wooden picture frame containing a blonde, pregnant woman and a much younger Christian.

In the photo, his hand draped over her swollen belly. Joy shone on his face.

"We should have never come here."

I grabbed his arm, stopping him from rising. The blanket pooled into a puddle on the floor, and he turned his head away. "Christian, it's not your fault."

"You don't understand. I wasn't here." His tongue ran along his lips. "I was on tour in Afghanistan."

"She drowned, didn't she?" I placed my hands on his jaw and forced him to look at me. "You saved me."

Christian shifted his gaze to my exposed body.

I bent down and covered myself with the fleece blanket.

Christian backed up. "Get dressed. I'll find something for us to eat." He whirled around and fled to the kitchen.

A cupboard slammed. I shimmied into the dry clothes and found him standing in front of the sink. The pond was in clear view through the window. "Christian?"

"Jenny was a figure skater. She spent most of her waking hours on the ice." He turned toward me. "Before I got deployed, we argued about her skating while pregnant."

"You couldn't have known what would happen."

"She didn't want—" His voice cracked.

I embraced him, and his arms curled around my back. "Jenny died knowing you loved her. There was nothing you could have done to stop her from going on that ice."

"Do you know it's been fifteen years since I've been here? You're the only person at the shelter who knows."

"Why me?"

"I wanted you to see you aren't the only one who's lost family. The reason I stay at the shelter is that they're my family now."

There was that word again, family. It was like Christian and Noel had conspired together to remind me what I no longer had. Being men, neither understood my innate desire for a child. Another chill wracked through me at the thought of never being a mother.

"Holly?" asked Christian.

"Hm?"

"You belong at the shelter, just like me. You may not have served in the service, but you have battle wounds like the rest—"

"What's for lunch? I'm hungry."

Christian removed a can from the pantry and set it on the countertop. He went to the fridge. "My favorite, tomato basil soup and three-cheese grilled cheese."

"Three-cheese grilled cheese?"

"Family secret," Christian jested. He slathered butter on the thick slices of baguette. "You can dump the tomato soup in the kettle and add milk."

"After lunch, I want to drive back to the shelter."

"Oh." Christian slowed his pace of slicing the cheddar cheese. He layered it over the bread. "I was hoping to take you on a sleigh ride this afternoon."

I whisked the milk and tomato soup together slowly, not responding to him.

"If that's what you want, we'll go back to Saint Aurora."

Twelve

I opened the oven and took out a pan of gingerbread men. The cookies refreshed their aroma in the kitchen each time they came out. I turned around and jerked, nearly dropping the hot cookie sheet onto the floor.

Eric stood at the island. He had come into the kitchen undetected while I was taking out the cookies. "Sorry," he said. He raised his chin and sniffed. "You're baking cookies this early in the morning?"

"Would you like one?"

"Can I?"

"Sit down and choose one."

Decorated and undecorated gingerbread men and women invaded the island's surface. Eric slumped into the chair. His eyes traveled cookie to cookie before selecting one. He broke off the gingerbread man's head. "Can't sleep?"

"Got a lot on my mind." Christian's reaction, after I had fallen through the ice, stayed with me. He said little on the drive home. My unsettled mind spun in circles, making sleep impossible. Baking had kept me occupied from thinking.

"These are fantastic," Eric mumbled. He chewed more and swallowed. "They remind me of the cookies in our Christmas packages while we were over there."

"Oh, that was nice of your grandma to send Christmas in a box. I'm sure it was difficult not being with your family during the holidays."

"It was a woman named Meredith Martin who'd send a little Christmas for the troops."

The bag of frosting in my hand slipped and splattered all over the floor. I leaned against the island. "What did you say?"

"Meredith Martin —"

"She's my mother." I studied his near black eyes. My voice dropped to a whisper, "She did that?"

Eric brushed his fingers off on a napkin. He pulled something out of his shirt pocket and unfolded it gingerly. It was a Christmas card that had been folded so many times, the creases were partially torn.

Though the handwriting was faded, the familiar curls and loops on the letters were Mom's. A lump lodged itself in my throat. All these years I never knew Mom sent Christmas packages overseas. I reached to touch the card.

Eric snatched it away. He folded and tucked it back inside his shirt pocket. "Your Mom's letters made us feel like family. After my grandma died, no one sent me mail in Iraq until Meredith."

"Not even your little brother?"

"He got involved with the gangs while I got out and joined the army."

"Why are you here?"

"The army discharged me six months ago. I went home, but found I wasn't welcome there, so came here because I wanted to find Meredith and thank her."

I blinked. Tears moistened my eyes. "She passed away last January from cancer."

"She wrote about you."

I dabbed my tears with a napkin. "She did?"

"Bragged about how proud she was of you and how much she prayed for you to find your family." Eric clasped my hand. "I hope you do too."

"Thanks," my voice fell below a whisper.

"'Tis the season for miracles," said Noel, peering through the doorway. He ambled over and wrapped an arm around me. "You've come to the right place for a family, and so did you, Eric."

I grabbed paper towels and knelt to clean the frosting mess off the floor.

The two men conversed while I wiped the frosting off the floor. Something inside me tossed around the word, family. I had never considered anyone family other than Deacon and Mom.

"Do you need help down here?" Noel squatted, holding a washcloth. He washed the sticky frosting remnants. "There, all clean." He smiled.

"Why does everyone keep talking about family?"

"Family is who's there for better and for worse. You, my child, are a beautiful addition to our shelter family."

I scoffed.

"Families come in different ways when you least expect it. After my son died, I never thought I'd feel the same way again until I met Christian."

Eric smacked his lips. "Mmm... mmm... mmm. Dang, that's good stuff. Can we mail some to my brothers?"

"Your brothers?" I tossed the paper towels into the garbage can.

"Yeah, the rest of my battalion is still in Iraq. I know they'd appreciate a little Christmas from the stateside."

"Oh, um—"

"It sounds like a great idea. In fact, I'll put up a list for those willing to write letters," said Noel.

Chloe waddled into the kitchen. "I thought I smelled gingerbread cookies. Wasn't sure if I dreamt it or not."

"Try one." Eric slid over a cookie.

Chloe nibbled on a leg. "This is amazing."

The clock beside the kitchen door showed five o'clock. One more hour left before the kitchen volunteers arrived to start breakfast. "We need to finish decorating the cookies and clean up," I said.

"I nominate we have gingerbread men for breakfast," Christian's baritone voice spoke.

I turned around and found him leaning against the back doorway.

Christian removed his gray beanie, black hair spilling to his shoulders. "Are there any left to go with coffee?"

Noel passed me. "I'll make coffee. Eric and Chloe, you finish decorating the cookies."

Christian and I stared at each other. He slipped off his jacket, hanging it on the back of a chair at the table. "How are you?"

"I'm fine."

The coffee maker trickled, its homey aroma dispersing in the air. Noel removed cups from the cupboard, clinking them together as he set them on the countertop. In the background Chloe and Eric talked with each other. Christian's blue eyes seemed to pierce through me.

I cleared my throat. "I learned that my mom mailed Christmas packages to the troops overseas. Eric suggested we do that here at the shelter."

"I know they'll appreciate it."

"Christian... I'm sorry about yesterday."

"Don't—"

Noel placed two coffee cups on the table. He returned with a plate of cookies, and when he left, Christian dunked his gingerbread man in the coffee. He swirled it. "It's my fault. I thought I was ready to face it."

Chloe laughed. It made me smile, and I glanced over at them. Eric and she attacked each other with frosting, each with globs smeared on their faces. Both stopped in a fit of giggles.

I sipped my coffee. "You want to get out of here? It seems they can finish up here without us."

Christian nodded. "I'll get our coffee to go."

"I'll be right back. Have to grab my stuff first." The chair protested being pushed from the table.

I entered the hallway.

"Holly," said Christian, glancing up and down the corridor.

Then his lips were on mine. I wrapped my arms behind his neck, and I pressed against him harder. Tingling sensations cascaded all over my body unlike anything I'd felt before— alive.

Christian severed the connection. His thumb stroked along my jaw, his gaze unwavering. "There's something between us."

"Yeah…" My voice came out husky. I brought my fingers to my lips.

"Us—"

"I know." I swallowed.

Christian turned his head, looking elsewhere other than me. "I don't think we should go anywhere together." He walked toward the lobby.

A throat cleared. Noel peeked from the kitchen doorway with a knowing smile. He winked. "Come join us for breakfast."

"I'll be there in a minute." I stared in a daze at the empty hallway where Christian had been seconds ago. Remembrance of our kiss made me tingle again. I couldn't recall the last time Deacon kissed me to that extent, if at all. Our love had died like Christian's wife.

A fresh cigarette smoke odor wafted behind me. Jared was the last person I wanted to see this morning. I stifled a groan and faked a smile. "Morning, Jared."

"Surprise," he said. "Was it you baking this morning?"

"What are you doing up?"

"Insomnia. I roam the building at night and, if I'm lucky, sneak out for a smoke."

Noel appeared in the doorway again. "Aw, I see Jared is also up early this morning. Would you like to join us for a breakfast of cookies?"

"Be my pleasure." Jared beamed a smile at me.

We joined the others in the kitchen and conversed while having coffee and gingerbread men. Christian never strayed far from my thoughts.

THIRTEEN

Christian swept the infirmary floor, while I inventoried the supplies in the cupboard. He hummed Christmas carols.

"Stop it."

Christian held the broom handle to his mouth like a microphone and burst into song. When he finished singing "Silent Night," he gave his half-grin. "Still not feeling Christmassy, huh?"

"It reminds me that my mom is gone."

"You said your mom loved Christmas, right?" asked Christian. He leaned the broom against the wall. "What better way to remember her than by celebrating the Christmas she loved?"

"I'm not ready." I clamped my bottom lip between my teeth and held it there.

"The livings rarely are," Christian said drily.

I shut the cupboard door. "I need fresh air."

"Want company?"

"No."

"Holly, remember what I said about an escort?"

"Fine, I'll just go to my room," I sighed.

Christian gazed into my eyes. "Promise me you won't go outside by yourself?"

"Yes," I whined.

"I don't trust that Jared. It always seems like he's lurking around wherever you are."

"Can I go to my room now without you lecturing me?"

"Yeah."

Christian locked the infirmary door behind us. While we waited for the elevator, he cleared his throat. "After my wife died, I hated the daily reminders too."

"Did she ruin Christmas for you?"

The elevator stopped on our floor. As we got on, Christian said, "She died on my birthday."

I did not respond. Nothing seemed right for a reply like that.

Christian stared ahead at the elevator doors. "A couple weeks later, after her funeral, I received a letter from Jenny," his voice went husky. "Inside were her latest ultrasound and a list of baby names she liked."

"I'm sorry," I whispered.

"Jenny's favorite was Noel."

The elevator opened to the women's floor. Christian's blue eyes seemed unwavering as he stood there.

I got off and turned around. "Thanks."

Before the doors slid shut, Christian said, "I don't want anything to happen to you."

I paced back and forth in my room thankful my roommate was gone. It would be another hour before supper. I had promised Christian I wouldn't, but the coiled energy within me demanded a walk outside. A short one couldn't hurt.

I snagged my jacket from the closet and made it through the shelter without running into Christian or Noel. Outside the front entrance, I discovered a loitering Jared. I spun around, hoping he wouldn't see me.

"Hiya, Holly," Jared's drawl stretched my name.

Too late. Maybe Jared isn't as bad as Christian thinks. That's why people came to the shelter, for a chance. Right?

Jared pulled a crumpled package from his coat pocket and removed a cigarette. He cupped his hand, lighting the end. "Smoke?"

I shook my head.

As Jared puffed, gray wisps trailed from his nose and mouth. A smoke cloud lingered. An orange ring glowed around the cigarette's end.

"You should quit," I said.

"Nah, it calms my nerves."

I shrugged. "I guess it's better than drugs."

"Your man?"

"I don't have one."

"Thought you were married? All the good ones are." Jared rolled out the lit end and shoved the unfinished cigarette in his pocket.

"Divorced." The word sounded strange yet. I wasn't sure how long it would take before it became part of my vocabulary.

"Recent?"

"Ho... how did you know?"

Jared crumpled the cigarette package in a ball. "The way you said it, like it was difficult to admit it."

I gave a harsh laugh.

Jared patted his coat pockets and searched through them, muttering something. He pulled out a cheap cellphone, texting something on it. "I need more cigarettes. Would you like to walk with me to the convenience store down the street?"

Christian's words niggled. I shoved my hands inside my coat pockets, and we started down the sidewalk past the shelter's bare trees. "What branch did you serve in?"

"The Marines, Ma'am."

"I suppose you're wondering how someone like me ended up in a veterans' homeless shelter."

Jared slowed his pace and glanced toward the street. "We all have our stories. After I got out, I got myself involved in a dangerous crowd."

"My ex-husband packed up his things and left me with nothing — no note, no money, and no apartment."

"I never wanted to do this." Jared shoved me in the direction of the shelter. "Run—"

A windowless black van screeched to a halt. Someone slid open the back door and jumped out on the sidewalk with a large gun. "Grab the woman and let's go," a man's voice ordered.

"She knows nothing." Jared pushed me behind him. The familiarity with which he spoke to the man shocked me. Christian was right.

"He will determine that himself." The stranger pointed the gun at him. "Now, hand her over."

Jared whispered, "Go."

I sprinted. Footsteps followed behind. My feet pushed harder against the pavement. A sharp ache began in my side, but I ignored it. Fingers wrapped around my arm, and I screamed. Gunshots pierced the air.

"Jared." I kicked and flailed at the body dragging me, their hold tightened with each attack.

Jared lay on the sidewalk, gasping.

The shooter stood over him with the gun aimed at him.

I shrieked, "N-o-o-o…"

My head flung backwards. A sickening crunch came from breaking his nose. An arm drew across my throat. "You little…"

Another gunshot fired, and I jerked. Hands shoved me forward into the van. My shins banged against the hard runners. "Get in there and shut up," the voice snarled.

Cold metal stung my cheek.

Someone's boot ground between my shoulder blades. They bounded my hands together until something plastic bit into my skin.

I squirmed. The noose around my wrists tautened.

A raucous laugh broke the silence. Someone pinched my butt, and I winced. His rank alcohol infused breath made me gag. "You'll pay for breaking my nose."

"Leave her alone. You can have your fun later when he's finished with her," said Jared's murderer.

Deacon. They wanted information on his whereabouts. My mouth dried. They would never believe that I knew nothing of Deacon's whereabouts. Perhaps I should lie. Either way, they planned on killing me.

The windowless walls of the van threatened to suffocate me. I closed my eyes. My stomach contents swirled like there were butterflies in it, threatening to spew if the movement didn't stop. "I'm going to be sick."

"Shut up." My captor slapped my face.

A vile taste in my mouth refreshed itself each time I swallowed. The van hit a pothole, and I vomited.

Expletives escaped from my future rapist's mouth. He seized my jaw, tracing it with the tip of a knife and pressing down until it broke the skin. Blood trickled down my throat.

"Please," I whimpered. "I don't know where Deacon is."

"That's for the boss to decide."

"Don't torture the poor girl yet, not until we get to the warehouse," said the shooter.

"She puked all over my shoes."

"I don't care, stick to the damn plan."

The toe of a boot jabbed me in the ribs, and I cried out.

"I said stop it." Gunfire went off, and a thud landed beside me.

Ringing in my ears crescendoed over the wild beating of my heart. Warm blood soaked into my jeans. The minutes stretched out in the darkness and I questioned if hours had passed since the shooting.

"Please don't kill me," I pleaded.

Nobody spoke, and I shivered. The one had mentioned torture. If I lived through this ordeal, I would be like the women in the support group.

After a while, my muscles ached from being in the same position too long. Time blurred together. How long had we been driving around? I kicked the sliding door.

"Stop that," shouted the murderer.

"I can't breathe. Get me out of here." I gasped short breaths. The van would swallow me alive before we arrived at my torture chamber. I recoiled at the pain in my sternum — the van's own form of torture. "Please!"

How long before Christian noticed my missing presence? I wriggled my hands, but it was no use.

The van's engine quit. The keys jangled, followed by a door slam. Oh God, this was it. The sliding door rolled open, clanking at the end of the track. I flinched. My arms jerked in a forced upward motion.

"On your feet," the killer hollered.

I twirled to the left and connected my head against his.

"You bitch," he yelled. The gun clattered against the pavement.

"Help," I shouted, staggering backward. The pavement jolted my body, and I screamed. Spots danced in circular motions in my vision. I rocked back and forth attempting to get up.

Footsteps ended near me. A choked sob mustered out of my throat. "Let me go."

"Tell me where Deacon is."

"I don't know."

My soon-to-be murderer carried me inside what appeared to be a warehouse. I squirmed. "Stop that," he snapped.

He deposited me on the floor in an empty room. The door slammed shut, reverberating.

FOURTEEN

The door banged louder with each kick. I leaned my forehead against the metal door, its coldness stinging my skin. "Let me out," my hoarse voice cracked.

Someone raised the volume level on the music that had been playing nonstop since my arrival. I was unsure if it had been mere hours or days. My headache pulsed in time with the bass notes.

"No. No. No," I begged, delivering a last kick.

My knees hit the floor, and I averted my gaze from the ceiling. The floodlights illuminated its relentless power above. My eyes burned. I wanted to go home.

The shelter was my home. I never pictured a homeless shelter being home. Both Noel and Christian were right.

I rested the back of my head against the wall. My eyelids struggled with staying open. A shrill screech intensified the ringing in my ears and my hands unable to cover them. "Stop," I screamed, my voice so hoarse it came out as a whisper.

The little spit I swallowed did nothing to satisfy my undying thirst. Is this what captured soldiers experienced? No wonder the women in our therapy group don't want to talk to me. I shuddered at the knowledge they had been tortured worse.

"Hang in there," said Christian. He appeared beside me.

"Christian? What are you doing here?"

"I'm here because you want me to be."

"Take me home."

"I'll be back."

"Wait." It was too late, he vanished. A dull ache formed behind my eyes, but no tears spilled.

The music turned off in the room. The silence amplified the tinnitus, and I tilted my ear toward the door. My heart raced. The door thudded against the wall, missing me.

A hand grabbed my hair and pulled. "Get up," he demanded.

The sharp pain made my eyes water. I squinted, trying to see past the blur for a better glimpse of my attacker.

The man gave a shove and sniggered.

I bit my tongue. A metallic tang erupted inside my mouth.

"I said, 'get up.'" He tugged my hair again.

"Why are you doing this?" I sobbed. "Deacon left me, and I don't know where he is."

Another man spoke. "Sit her on the chair."

That damn wooden chair. If I ever got freed, I wanted to smash it against the floor and walls until splinters remained. My tormentor dragged me across the room.

My rear slammed into the fragmented seat, the slivers poking through my pants. I squirmed, the splinters digging into my flesh a little more.

"Are you thirsty?" The stranger waved a water bottle in front of my face.

I nodded.

He twisted open the cap.

My tongue snagged on my cracked lips. The man wore a dark peacoat with black trousers and dress shoes. I strained my eyes, trying to make out his facial features.

"Where's my money?"

My gaze traveled to the water bottle. "No idea."

The water bottle tipped upside down and cascaded onto the concrete floor. Water. I jerked. The chair screeched with the repetitive movements. My lips smacked. His henchman held me back.

"Uh uh." He wagged his finger and continued pouring. The bottle empty, the boss tossed it aside by the puddle. "Let's try again. Where is Deacon?"

Water. The pool on the floor grew thinner. Need water. Jared's murderer grabbed my jaw and applied pressure.

"I-I-I don't know," I whimpered. They would kill me whether I knew where Deacon was or not. Christian, where are you? Goosebumps rippled up and down my arms at the prospect of never seeing him again.

"Tell him," a low voice rumbled.

"He left me with nothing."

"Where is he?" the well-dressed man shouted within inches of my face.

I winced at the loudness.

His nose brushed against mine, and he shouted the question again.

"He... he... didn't say."

"Get the pitcher and towel."

The pressure released off my jaw. My wrists strained against the zip ties and I hit the chair. A palm cracked across my cheek. "Stop that. Now tell me where your husband is?"

"Ex," I screamed until it felt like thousands of razor blades slit the inside of my throat.

A clank jiggled across a metal cart. On top, it contained multiple tools, all various sizes, used in plying information out of people. This only happens in the movies, right? My stomach churned. They would use them on me. They would never believe me about Deacon's whereabouts.

"Tip her back."

The murderer followed the order.

"You have information on Deacon." His boss draped a towel over my face. "Now tell me what it is."

"I'm telling you the truth!"

Ice rattled inside the pitcher. Coldness flooded over me, and I gasped, sucking in the water. A coughing fit refused to cease. "I... don't... know..." I wheezed.

"You know something."

More water pummeled in what seemed to be a never-ending waterfall. I'm going to die. I'm supposed to die as an old lady surrounded by her children and grandchildren, not with two murderers.

Oxygen. Can't... breathe...

I sputtered, shivering. So c-c-cold.

He yelled more. Each time I answered nothing, he dumped more water. My lungs burned.

"Boss. Let her sit for a few more hours."

"Christian," I muttered. "Christian."

Someone removed the wet towel. "What did you say?"

"She said, 'Christian.'"

My eyelids refused to open past a slit. Sleep. I wanted to sleep in a nice warm bed. A clicking sound repeated itself. Wait. That's my teeth chattering.

Someone gave a hard shove, and I landed on the wet floor. The tools clanked against the metal cart. The door slammed.

Maybe they believed me now. I lay in the water puddle, my body too heavy to withstand any movement.

The floodlights hummed. Music played again, and I groaned.

"Drink," said Christian.

I opened my eyes.

Christian pointed at the water puddle. "Drink."

"I… I… I can't."

"Yes, you can. You're a survivor."

"I want to be at home with you."

Christian dunked his hand in the puddle and let the water drip off his fingers. "Soon. Now drink."

I grunted as I adjusted my position. The tip of my tongue stuck out, and I paused. This is so gross. Don't think about germs. I slurped the water off the floor at first, then faster with each gulp, relieving my parched throat and mouth.

Christian was gone. I found him nowhere in the room and panicked. His presence had calmed me. Dampness seeped through my coat and shirt.

"Looking for me?" Christian whispered near my ear. I flinched.

"You need to get out of the water."

I rolled over and sat in an upright position, tucked my legs underneath. One... two... three. I rose from the floor. "I did it."

"Christian? I did—" No one else was in the room.

The music stopped. A loud growl from my stomach filled the void. A different music genre started, and I screamed. My hands twisted and turned in several directions in their bonds. My shoulders ached.

I placed my wrists together and sighed. The zip tie snapped. Freedom had arrived when I least expected it. I winced at my newfound ability to move my arms. Bloodied rub marks had tattooed themselves around my wrists.

The wooden chair taunted me. I kicked it and sent it skittering across the room. At its resting place, I picked up the chair, the slivers prickling. I dropped the chair. Fresh blood droplets spilled onto the floor. Ignoring the new pain, I gripped the chair legs and hurled it all against the wall. The pieces splintered.

I tossed a spindle at the floodlight. "Let me out."

It missed the light and hit the floor with a clatter. I dropped to my knees, sobbing.

A louder tune played.

I curled into a fetal position and covered my ears. "Christian, where are you?" I whimpered.

FIFTEEN

Grit renewed itself with every blink as I lay on the floor. No music. The floodlights hummed over the silence. Male voices shouted.

"No," I said, striking against an arm.

It proved fruitless. Someone lifted me onto something cold and hard and forced me flat on my back. I bucked against him. Fingers dug farther into my skin. Another man draped a strap below my chest and tightened it.

I kicked. "Stop it."

The two men repeated the same procedure with my legs. I squeezed my eyes closed. "You ready to tell me where Deacon is?" asked someone.

"I don't know."

"Fine, if you won't tell me on your own perhaps a needle under your fingernail will."

"I—"

A point poked my nail bed, and I jerked.

"I'm sorry, what was that?" he asked, jabbing it farther.

"I woke up and found Deacon gone—"

The tip pushed in deeper. Blood trickled inside my mouth from where I had bitten my tongue. If I didn't, I would scream.

"Where did he take my money?"

Christian spoke. "Lie. He doesn't believe you're telling the truth, so lie. It'll keep you alive longer."

"Where are you?"

"I'm coming—"

I screamed. Something had thrust farther in my nail bed and remained stuck there. I could make out nothing beyond the bright lights.

"Give me Deacon," the man shouted.

"The money…"

"Yeah?" His voice was eager.

"… is with him." I clenched my jaw.

My torturer struck me across the face. "Give me another needle."

"It's at the shelter." The words burst through my lips.

The needle clinked. He withdrew the other beneath my nail. Footsteps stopped. "Do whatever you want with her."

"Thanks, boss." Jared's murderer gave a sinister chuckle. A gun barrel jammed against my forehead. "First, I will let you sleep before the fun begins."

"Please…"

His palm pressed against my lips. "Quiet now."

Each floodlight powered off one at a time until darkness descended in the room. I wriggled, but the straps did not budge. My eyes rolled back in my head. "Must stay awake."

I jerked my chin forward and the back of my head hit the table with a bang. The longer I lay there, the more I became unsure if my eyes were open or closed.

A sharp edge sliced across my belly. I gritted my teeth. My heavy eyelids opened a slit, enough to witness the horror he intended on inflicting. It was another game. I should have known he would never let me sleep.

He jabbed with a fingertip. "Wake up."

Goosebumps coursed up my arms. It wouldn't matter whether I answered because he planned on killing me slow. I took shallow breaths.

His fingers unfastened the buttons on my coat until he reached the strap. He positioned the knife tip against the base of my throat. The other hand fidgeted with the strap, unfastening it. Clothing layers were peeled back, exposing my breasts.

"Pretty skin." A fingertip swirled around a breast, stopping at its puckered nipple. He repeated it on the other. "Beautiful."

I shivered. His tone was like the criminals on the cop shows.

He placed the flat, frosty blade against my skin, and I stifled a gasp. The sharp end tipped slightly. It stung as he dragged the knife, pressing harder. Blood trickled down my stomach and side.

"Please…" I pleaded. "Let me go. I promise I won't—"

He lifted the knife. "What, don't you want to have fun with me?"

The knife tip pricked between my breasts. He skimmed it downward. When it reached my jeans, he laid the knife on the table's edge and unbuttoned my pants. I fought against the straps.

As he unzipped my zipper, I cringed at its grating noise. Oh God, he plans on raping me. I stiffened. This is how Chloe felt — powerless.

He leaned forward and tugged, sliding my jeans enough to expose my underwear. My soon-to-be rapist picked up the knife. He slithered the knife along my panty line.

The door burst open. "Drop the knife," shouted a man.

A clatter echoed against the floor. "Interlace your fingers behind your head and on your knees."

A black uniform stood over Jared's murderer, handcuffing him, I assumed.

"Holly," said Christian's baritone voice.

"Are you real?" I sobbed.

Christian undid the straps. Tears washed over my face as he dressed me. He lifted me against his chest and the scent of candy orange slices filled my nose. His body was warm and real. Fingers touched a bruise on my jaw. "We need to get you to the hospital."

"No." I gripped his shirt collar. His blue eyes peered into mine. "I want to go home."

"Holly, you need x-rays and an IV. A doctor needs to check you over."

"You're a doctor."

"The infirmary is not equipped for that stuff." Christian carried me out of my prison. Two paramedics and a gurney waited outside the door.

I clutched his shirt and begged, "Please."

Christian untangled my fingers, talking in a soothing tone. "It's okay, I'm here."

I screamed as the gurney collided with my back. A blanket covered my shaking body.

Christian held out a hand toward a paramedic. "I'll put her IV in."

The tip of the needle punctured, and I yanked it away. "That hurts. I hate needles."

"Look at me. Let's get you to the hospital and if you don't have any major injuries, I promise I will bring you home."

"I… I… I had to lick water off the floor." I turned my head away, refusing to see the disgust on his face.

Christian touched my cheek. "You survived. It doesn't matter what you did to stay alive." His sugar-coated lips lightly kissed my cheek. "Let's load her."

"You're… done with my IV?" Plastic tubing trailed from the medical tape. "But I didn't feel anything."

Christian gave his half-smirk. He walked alongside as the paramedics pushed the gurney outside. A frigid wind blew through the blanket. I shivered. The fresh chill revived my thankfulness that I survived.

The ambulance doors slammed shut. I squeezed Christian's hand and whispered. "Get me out of here."

"Focus on me, not the ambulance."

"How did you find me?"

"Jared."

"He's alive?"

Christian shook his head. "It was too late. The cops pulled information off his phone."

"I'm tired."

Christian tapped my hand. "Keep talking."

"How long?"

"Almost three days. Chloe saw you and Jared leave the grounds. When you didn't come back, she became worried."

My eyelids drooped.

"Come on, stay awake a little longer." Christian shook my hand.

"Music."

A finger pried my eyelids open, and a light shone back and forth. "Keep talking."

"Turn it off," I mumbled.

"Holly?"

Sixteen

Sunlight and the vertical blinds battled over the lighting inside the room. Machines hummed near my head. A dry erase board hung on the wall across the room with my name written at the top. I patted myself and winced.

Chloe slept in a chair beside the bed. Someone had draped a blanket over her and secured the corners behind her shoulders.

"She's awake." Christian stood at the bed's footboard with a coffee cup in his hand.

"Where am I?"

"The hospital."

Chloe yawned, stretching her arms upward. "Welcome back."

Someone knocked at the door. A large flower bouquet covered the person's face. "Delivery for Holly Bradford," said a familiar man's voice, one I had spent twelve years married to.

I gasped.

Deacon winked as he set them on the bedside table. "You're a lucky lady."

"Thanks…"

"I hope you have a fast recovery." Deacon smiled and made his departure.

"Ooh, who sent flowers?" asked Chloe. She plucked the card from its pick holder and opened it. Her eyes skimmed over the words several times then flipped it over, looking at the other side. "Who is apologizing to you?"

"Deacon."

Christian sprinted into the hallway after him.

"Did the police make an arrest?" I croaked.

"One, but he's not talking," said Chloe. Her hand flew to her mound, and she groaned. When the pain subsided, she rubbed her belly. "I hate Braxton-Hicks."

"When is your estimated due date?"

"The week of Christmas. Why did you let him go?"

"I don't know."

"Someone should be here to get your statement. What happened?"

I picked at the tape on top of my hand. "I don't want to talk about it. Why are you here?"

"Because you've been here for me, so I returned the favor."

My captor's voice echoed inside my mind. "Where's my money?"

"The shelter." I ripped the IV needle out of my hand and threw back the blanket covers.

Chloe exclaimed in protest.

"He — the shelter's in danger."

"From whom?"

The tiled floor was cool under my bare feet. I tore through the closet for my clothes and shoes. "The other kidnapper." They weren't there. I tried the dresser drawers below the TV.

"Stop. The police will take care of it."

"Not if they don't know about him," I argued.

"She's right," said Pete, entering the room. "Can you describe him?"

I closed my eyes, only a blurred face appeared. "All I can see is his coat. It's a dark color pea coat, black I think."

Pete pulled a pen and pad from his coat pocket and wrote something. His usual uniform was gone, and in its place, he wore black business attire. "Is there anything else you can remember that can help us identify him?"

I shivered at the reminder. "Only that Deacon owed him money."

"Holly… this is difficult, but I have to ask how he tortured you."

I pulled a sweater from the clothing bag I had found in the bottom drawer. Someone had replaced my dirty clothes with clean ones. I clenched the sweater against my chest. "I can't," I whispered.

"Please, anything you can tell me might help us figure out who this guy is."

I shook my head.

Pete closed the pad cover and shoved it along with the pen in his pocket. He took a step forward.

I flinched. "Don't."

"Call me if you think of anything else."

"I'll see that she does," said Chloe.

"I'm sorry this happened to you, Holly. Talk to someone, because if you don't—"

"I'm fine," I said.

"I'll keep you updated."

Christian loomed in the doorway. "Pete, you're here. We need to talk." He gestured toward the hallway.

They mentioned Deacon in their hushed conversation. Pete glanced at me. My ex-husband had hurt me by leaving the way he did, but he would want no harm to come to me.

I yanked on the sweater and grabbed jeans out of the bag. "Why are you focusing on Deacon? He's not the one who kidnapped me."

Christian and Pete stopped talking.

"We were married for twelve years. Now, come on, you're wasting time."

Christian crossed his arms across his chest. "Where do you think you're going?"

"Home."

"Holly…" His voice rumbled. "Stay here a little longer."

"No, I'm going home."

Christian caught my wrist but did not squeeze. His blue eyes gazed into mine. "Where's home?"

"The shelter. Now, are you and Chloe coming?" I leaned to put on my boots and gritted my teeth. My bruises and scrapes would fade over time, but would the memory of what my kidnappers had done? I rubbed my ribs.

"I'm gonna find someone to prepare your discharge papers."

"Fine."

Pete went with Christian, leaving me alone with Chloe. I shuffled to the bathroom and stood in front of the mirror. Ugly bruises had formed on my face. The woman in the mirror also moved her hand. She and I were the same person. I swallowed.

"Are you okay?" asked Chloe.

I gave a startled gasp.

Chloe hesitated. She took a cautious step. "You're safe now."

"I should have trusted him."

"Who, Christian?"

Tears moistened my eyes with each blink. "I didn't heed his warning to stay away from Jared, because I thought it was jealousy."

"This was not your fault. It's your ex-husband's addiction."

"I just want to go home and forget about all this."

"You won't. It always stays in the back of your mind." Chloe pointed at her swollen belly. "It's been almost nine months and I still relive it most days."

"Being raped and being tortured for information are two different things," I snapped.

"And you don't think I was in pain when he forced himself in me? Wow…" Chloe turned around. "Until you've been raped, don't tell me it's not the same thing." She marched out of the bathroom.

"I'm sorry. I didn't know."

No response. When I searched for Chloe, I found she had left my hospital room.

Christian stormed through the door. "What did you say to her?"

"I made a mistake. She told me she understood what it was like remembering…"

"Let me tell you something about Chloe. If anyone understands what you've been through, it'd be her. Not only did her commanding officer abuse his power, he covered it up by making it look like insurgents did it."

"I… I didn't know."

"Let's go. Your paperwork has been taken care of, but they need your signature at the nurses' station." Christian removed my coat from the closet and held it open like a gentleman.

"Thank you for the clean clothes."

"Thank Chloe. She's the one who thought about it." He motioned toward the door. "Shall we?"

We stopped by the nurses' station. I signed discharge papers stating I was being released in Christian's care. Afterwards, I jammed my hands in my coat pockets and walked beside him in silence.

The elevator opened, and someone exited. We rushed, getting in as the door began closing.

Christian tapped his fingers against his jeans. "Did you hallucinate about me while you were held hostage?"

I stared at him. "Maybe."

"I knew it."

In the hospital lobby Chloe paced. She averted her gaze when we approached.

"I'll bring the truck round," said Christian.

I forced a small smile. "We'll watch for you."

Chloe and I stood near the sliding glass doors, her back facing me. "I'm sorry," I said.

"Christian's here." She brushed past without waiting.

I blinked. An apology was not enough. Underneath her tough exterior, I had wounded her. It would take more than a simple apology to restore our friendship. The ride home would be unbearable.

Seventeen

Noel sipped his coffee while reading the newspaper at the island in the kitchen. The newspaper crinkled. Noel peered off to the side of it and smiled. "Morning, Holly."

"Morning." I removed the half-empty pot from the coffeemaker and poured a cup.

"How are you feeling today?"

"Sore."

"Pete recruited some off-duty deputies and stationed them around the shelter." Noel resumed reading the newspaper. "The ladies are expecting you this morning."

"I… I can't."

"Yes, you can." Noel folded the newspaper and set it beside his syrup covered plate. "You all need each other's support, especially you."

"I won't talk about it."

"Then go listen."

I sighed. Why couldn't he leave me alone?

The chair scuffed across the floor. His palms pressed against the table. Noel spoke, "I know you think we're being hard on you about opening up, but we're concerned about you. We're a family here."

"I'm fine, really."

"You don't believe it though. Come, I'll walk with you."

I topped off my coffee mug. We walked out of the kitchen and down the hallway without speaking to each other. As people met in passing, Noel greeted them with a nod and smile.

There they were. Through the window, the ladies in the support group smiled and laughed as they visited with one another. It was like they had forgotten anything bad had happened to them.

Chloe sat near the back, talking with Lisa. She had avoided me since my return from the hospital. Our eyes met. She turned her head away. I stepped back from the window. "I can't go in there."

"Yes, you can." Noel faced me. "Do you know why?"

I shook my head.

"You're a survivor, just like these women. Now, get in there." Noel pushed open the door. "Good morning, ladies. Holly is back."

The chatter and laughter died. One by one the women's smiles disappeared, and they gawked. An awkward silence emerged.

I wasn't sure if being kidnapped and tortured counted enough by their definition of being one of them. Violence had impacted our lives.

Still, I was unsure what to say. I studied them through fresh eyes, like I saw them for the first time. The silent seconds stretched further into uneasiness.

At last Chloe rose. "Would you like to start?"

I swallowed. "No." My voice came out foreign, lower than a whisper, and one I had never heard before today.

Noel patted my shoulder and murmured, "You can do it."

As he exited the room, I willed myself not to follow. I took a swig of coffee, but it did not relieve my dry mouth. "I, uh… have nothing to say…"

Chloe folded her arms across the top of her mound. "You were abducted."

"What do you want me to say?"

"How did you feel?"

I slumped into an empty chair. "I'm fine."

"I'll start then." Chloe seated herself in the chair she had been sitting in earlier. Her lips pressed together and parted several times. "Many of you know I was raped, but I've never told anyone what he did afterwards. He strung me up like an animal and beat me until he was sure I would die."

Chloe gave a wry laugh. "The joke's on him, because a day later, another troop found me barely alive. After I was treated and released from the hospital, I pretended everything was fine at first. Later, I found out I was pregnant," her voice dropped.

Everyone leaned forward at the edge of their chairs.

Chloe remained quiet for a minute. "All the emotions I had pushed so hard to forget the last twelve weeks came tumbling out. I never saw a doctor until meeting Dr. Hunt here at the shelter. He convinced me I have choices — avoidance or acceptance, but one needed to be chosen."

"Which one did you choose?" I asked with a whisper.

"I'm working on acceptance."

Tears obstructed my view. I closed my eyes to staunch them, but they continued falling. "I'm so sorry." My voice cracked, followed by another sob.

Everything I had struggled with keeping inside, jumbled around in a mess. My throat burned. Claws seemed to have gripped around my head, making it ache. Each time my crying let up, I'd get a mental glimpse of the men hurting me, and I cried harder.

Arms wrapped around me. Another set joined followed by several more until I became entangled in the center of a group hug.

I sniffled. "Thanks."

All the warmth stripped away with each woman disentangling herself.

"I'm sorry too," said Chloe, the last woman still embracing me.

"They wouldn't believe me," I babbled.

"Bad guys rarely do. Maybe it's because they spend too much time lying themselves."

The shrill fire alarm screamed. "He's here," I whimpered.

"It's just a fire drill," someone commented.

Chloe cracked the door. Gunfire ricocheted its echoes down the hallway. She shut it. "Do any of those windows open?"

Nobody answered.

Chloe clapped and raised her voice. "We're sitting targets here. Move."

Lisa and another woman banged against the two windows in the room, neither budged. "Get the chair," Lisa ordered.

Chloe gestured a signal, which I assumed in the military meant something like be quiet. She eased open the door, making it appear closed. An eerie quiet hovered. She pressed her ear against the slight opening.

The door opened farther, and Chloe stuck her head out. "It's clear." She resumed an upright position. "Somebody needs to sneak down the hallway and check things out."

A few women cowered behind their chairs. Others stood motionless. They had survived war overseas only to have their home attacked. It was my fault.

"I'll go."

"Are you sure, Holly?" Chloe asked.

"I did this, and I have to be the one to clean it up."

The door closed behind. I tiptoed, hugging the wall, inch by inch in what seemed like a mile of hallway.

Near the kitchen, a man's voice carried from the lobby. He wanted money. It's him, the man in the peacoat!

I froze. My stomach roiled at each word he spoke. I gagged upon remembering what he had done to me. A hand covered my mouth, and another wrapped around my waist, snatching me inside the kitchen. The person muffled my scream.

"Shh." Christian whispered in my ear. His orange cologne comforted me, and I relaxed. He removed his hand. "I called the police fifteen minutes ago."

"Where's Noel?"

"He's talking to the guy."

"We have to do something."

Christian glanced at the clock hanging beside the doorway. "The SWAT team should be in place."

"We can't wait for them." I scanned the kitchen for anything I could use for a weapon. My gaze stopped on top of the island. "The knife set."

"What's your plan?"

I withdrew a paring knife. My fingertip traveled the length of its sharpened edge. "Get close enough and stab him. We need a bag and something heavy enough that feels like money."

Christian's blue eyes met mine. "I know what you're thinking, and it won't work. You don't have enough strength."

"Then you do it."

"I won't kill him." Christian gently pried the knife out of my clutch.

"I don't want him dead. Just hurt enough to wish it."

Shouts followed by multiple crashes traveled from the lobby. Glass shattered, and I jerked. "What's happening?"

The paring knife clinked against the island. "Either someone was a hero, or it's the SWAT team. My guess is the latter."

"What if it's not?" A chill rippled through my arms and the back of my neck.

"It is."

Heavy boot steps entered the kitchen. They belonged to a man who stood as tall as Christian. He wore all black except for the white letters across his chest identifying him as SWAT. "You Christian? Pete said you were in here."

"Yeah, and this is Holly."

"Will you come with me and tell us if it's the man who held you hostage?"

My insides quivered, and I closed my eyes. Did I want to face my tormentor? Some part within wished it was someone else who had attacked the shelter. A dull ache started in my jaw. I released the tension I had unknowingly clenched.

"Holly?" It was Christian who spoke my name, but I wasn't sure. His fingers caressed my cheek. "I'll be with you."

I cupped my hand over Christian's and opened my eyes.

"Follow me," said the man in black.

The farther we left the kitchen's sanctuary, the more my insides jiggled. Each step became heavier. I stumbled forward, and Christian caught me.

"If I didn't know better, I'd say you were looking for an excuse for me to carry you again," he teased.

But I did. I wanted to be carried away rather than face what was in the lobby. Noel would kick me out after learning I had put the shelter in danger. We continued.

Around the corner, my feet failed again, and I staggered. I rubbed my eyes in case they had deceived me the first time. They hadn't. Not only did my captor stand there in handcuffs, so did my ex-husband. "Deacon? What are you doing here?"

"Protecting you. I couldn't let him hurt you for something I did," Deacon replied.

"Why?"

"I never thought they'd go after you. Not until I heard about your kidnapping—"

"Don't." I turned away from him. "Get him out of my sight."

The other prisoner sneered.

Clarity did nothing in identifying this man except for his peacoat, which I couldn't be sure of. I shook my head. "I-I-I don't know."

If it was him, the trial hinged on his co-conspirator's testimony and evidence police had collected at the warehouse. Christian wrapped an arm around my shoulder. "Don't worry, he'll be found guilty for something."

EIGHTEEN

Silent Night" came on over the radio. I gripped the pot, its red foiled paper crinkling under my fingers. The cab driver glanced in his rear-view mirror. "What's your favorite carol?"

In the window's reflection, I fought for composure. "I don't know."

"This song is my daughter's favorite. She's been practicing it for her school concert."

"It was my mom's favorite too."

The cemetery came into view. Snow covered both the tops and bottoms of the headstones, leaving a slight color in-between. The stark white contrasted with the tall black fence spindles outlining the graveyard perimeter.

"You can drop me off here."

The cab driver parked in front of the gate's entrance. I removed cash from my wallet and paid him. His arm straddled across the seat. "Hope you enjoy your holidays."

"Thanks." I shut the cab door.

The cab pulled away and blended in with the traffic.

Snow crunched under each step I took. Drifts covered the ground in varying layers, making it difficult to locate my mother's grave. I paused. A pine tree marked her plot, a condition she had included in her burial plans. 'Her year-round Christmas tree,' she said.

The chiseled letters of my mother's name stood bleak against the dark granite. No cake marked her birthday celebration today. I pressed my lips together. If I didn't, the pent-up grief behind my eyes would not stop once it began.

A poinsettia sat atop her grave marker, its blooms, silky between my fingers. Snowflakes flittered from the gray sky. "I miss—" I gave a choked sob.

The cold breeze nipped at the silent tears on my cheeks. I wrapped my arms around myself. A rumble on the cemetery road slowed to a stop until the engine idled. Someone slammed a car door.

A hand touched my shoulder. "I miss her too."

"Noel. How did you know I'd be here?"

"It's her birthday today." Noel laid a dozen red roses next to the poinsettia plant and stared at the headstone. "Letting her go is a regret I have."

"What are you saying?"

Noel pulled a folded envelope out of his coat pocket. "Meredith sent me this letter when she was in the hospital."

"Why would she send you a letter?" I gawked at the red envelope in his hand. When had she written it? I had stayed by her bedside day and night.

Noel licked his lips. "Holly… you're my daughter."

"No… it's impossible. I don't have a father."

"Do you remember the story I told you at the courthouse? That woman was your mother."

I took a step backward. "She never told me. Why wouldn't she have told me?"

Keys jingled. "Meredith has a safety deposit box at your bank. All the answers are there, whenever you are ready."

"I imagined for so long what my father was like," I whispered.

For thirty-five years, I had watched older men and wondered if my father was amongst them. My mother explained my father's absence by saying that he was a sperm donor. Until now, I had assumed it meant she used a fertility clinic and left the matter alone.

"I couldn't believe it was you that day I met you."

"Did you follow me to the diner?"

Noel's cheeks reddened, and he shook his head. "Not on purpose. Say, you want to go to the diner?"

"Nah, I should get going."

"Not even for German chocolate cake?" The corners of his lips gave a twitch. "That was Meredith's favorite."

I shrugged. "Why now?"

"She was worried about you." Noel motioned his head toward the pickup.

I tucked the deposit box keys inside my jeans pocket and walked beside him. "I meant where were you when she lay dying in the hospital?"

"Carrying on her work for the troops overseas. She had the letters written and entrusted me with sending them in the packages."

"Wait." I stopped. "You knew about it already and said nothing?"

"She wasn't trying to hide it from you, and neither was I."

"Then why?"

"You've been stressed with all that's happened — losing your job and home, the divorce — I didn't want to add more." Noel reached for my hand.

I swatted it away. "Don't."

"Holly…"

"Leave me alone." I continued down the road.

The truck matched my pace. Noel leaned over and cracked the passenger window. "Come on, get in. I'll take you to the bank."

"Why, so you can tell me what other secrets Mom kept from me?"

"You and she are more alike than you know. Family meant everything to her too."

I hesitated.

Noel parked the pickup. "Your mom had so much love that she shared with those less fortunate than you." He swung open the door. "Please get in."

The heat blasted on high against my hands. I snuck glimpses at Noel. One by one, his facial features resembled my own. Throughout the years, many people were surprised Mom and I were mother and daughter because we looked nothing alike.

"Yes, I had red hair at one time." Noel chuckled.

"Why didn't you approach us that day?"

"At the time, I was confused and angry at the idea that she might have had an affair resulting in a child. It never occurred to me you were my daughter."

"What did you do afterwards?"

"I tried to move on, but it didn't go as I'd intended because money can't bring you happiness. My second wife took my son and divorced me, eventually." Noel relaxed his arm along the window ledge.

"Did you have a helper named Marley?"

A deep laugh emanated from him. "Something similar happened."

The left blinker clicked repeatedly while we waited for a clearing between cars. Noel eased into the bank's parking lot, circling it several times. No empty spots available, Noel dropped me off at the entrance.

I straightened my jacket and pulled on the partially frosted glass door. An older male guard held the second door. "Welcome to Minnesota First Bank."

Fresh pine permeated the lobby, though no tree stood in view. Silver garland and lights decorated the tellers' countertops. Christmas bulbs dangled from the ceiling.

"How may I assist you today?" asked a young woman, drumming her fingertips against the counter.

"I'm here to access Meredith Martin's safety deposit box."

"Name and id please."

"Holly Bradford."

She took my id. The keyboard clacked as she entered information into the computer. Her eyes scanned what was on the monitor. "You are on the list. Follow me."

The room containing the safety deposit boxes seemed quiet compared to the lobby. The woman faced the metal doors and muttered, "One two two four."

She located it, inserted her key, and twisted it until it clicked. "Your turn."

My key fell on the carpeted floor. "Sorry," I mumbled.

My trembling fingers couldn't grasp it despite several tries. I took a deep breath and released it slowly. On the last attempt, I retrieved the key.

I placed the key in the lock and turned it. The cover flipped open.

The teller removed the box and placed on the table. "When you're finished, let someone know."

"Wait, I'd like to empty it and take home the contents."

"Do you want to close out the account?"

"Yes." I peeked inside. Mom had used a safety deposit box for a single envelope. Her curlicue handwriting embellished my name across the front. I missed it.

"I'll get the paperwork."

Alone, I sniffed the envelope. Any trace of Mom's vanilla perfume was long gone. My fingernail slid underneath the flap. I removed several letters, written front and back, from within and stared at the first page without seeing the words.

A sniffle sounded. I folded the papers and tucked them back inside the envelope, slipping it in my purse.

The woman teller returned. She laid a document and pen on the table and pointed at the signature line. "Sign and date here."

When we finished, she escorted me to the lobby and returned to her post.

I stood in the middle of the atrium — customers walked past — and embraced Mom's spirit. She must have known she was dying long before she told me. I adjusted my purse strap and took one more look at the Christmas decorations.

In the parking lot, I craned my neck, searching for Christian's beat up truck. A short toot came from the back of the lot. I jammed my hands into my pockets and started towards Noel.

Noel met me halfway. I climbed into the pickup and slammed the door shut.

"Back so soon?" Noel asked.

"I couldn't bring myself to read it." I faced the passenger side window. "Just drive."

Nineteen

The morning sun spilled its rays into the courtyard, forcing back the nighttime darkness one section at a time. Dawn was Mom's favorite part of the day. She often sat on our apartment balcony, with a coffee cup in her hands, watching the sunrise. When asked why, she would respond with 'I like facing all my day's troubles first thing.'

I never understood her method, but today seemed like the day to learn. Her letter crinkled under my fingertips. My mouth dried. These were her last words. If I put off reading them, maybe her death wouldn't seem so final.

I placed the papers beside me on the bench. Hot liquid sloshed over the edges of my coffee cup, and onto her last words. I snatched up the letter. The coffee dripped off and onto the sidewalk.

Her pristine handwritten words blurred together. I squinted at the words within the wet spot.

Life has no guarantees, only regrets.
It is too late for me to face my regrets, but

not for you. I know your heart's desire is to have your own family. Because of my selfishness, you never learned that families don't necessarily share blood relations to be family…

I shuddered. She was wrong. Mom was the least selfish person always sure my needs were met or willing to cover a co-worker's shift.

I skimmed the next paragraph for a further explanation, angling the paper several ways. A loud sigh made its escape. It was no use. The ink had bled into an illegible blob.

"Troubles?" asked Dylan.

I jerked. His usual shuffling noise had snuck up on me "I spilled coffee on my letter before I read it."

"Want me to try?"

"No!" I folded the letter. "I mean — no thanks."

"You sure? It looks important."

"It's fine." I nestled the letter back inside the envelope and stuck it in my coat pocket. "What are you doing out here?"

Dylan slouched on the bench beside me. "My morning walk to the old bench here." He stared, like he was studying my face. "Your bruises are fading."

"Make-up."

"You did a good job covering them. How are you feeling?"

I scoffed. "Why does everybody keep asking me that?"

"We're worried about you."

"It's been a horrible month and I just want it to be over with, so I can move on with my life."

"I see. And how are you planning to move on?"

"I... I... I'm not sure," I replied. What were my plans? Get a job and an apartment?

"Stay here for a while, at least until after Christmas." Dylan's brown eyes never wavered.

"Did Noel put you up to this?"

Dylan shook his head. "You've become family. If it wasn't for this place, I wouldn't have anybody."

"What about your two boys?"

"I haven't seen them in two years."

"What? Why?"

"They don't need to see me like this. Who wants a dad who's homeless?"

Tears bubbled up to the surface, and I blinked. I squeezed his hand. "Trust me. They won't care because all they want is their dad."

Noel appeared in the window.

"I know because I never had a dad when I was growing up. But I do now."

"My ex-wife probably wouldn't allow me to see them."

"Call her."

"I might." Dylan glanced at Noel.

"Excuse me. I need to talk with him."

"He's your dad, isn't he?"

I nodded. "He told me yesterday."

"Go talk."

I gripped the coffee cup's handle. We hadn't spoken since yesterday after leaving the bank. How am I supposed to address him — Noel or Dad?

Noel held the door, his inviting smile never straying. "Morning. Did you get all your troubles sorted?"

The shelter's heat was welcomed. I stomped my boots upon the weathered rug. A chill rippled through my body, and I shuddered. The outside temperature hadn't seemed cold until coming inside.

"Hot coffee, if you want it." Noel raised an extra cup.

Though the hot beverage warmed my stomach, it did little at warding off the cold that settled within my core. I took another long swallow. "Thanks. How did you know I was here?"

"You are your mother's daughter. I figured you'd wait till morning to read her letter."

"It's ruined."

Noel tipped his head.

I placed the cup on the buffet table resting against the windowpane, and unzipped my jacket pocket, removing the envelope. "I can't read it."

Noel slipped out the folded papers with ease. He took his time prying apart the melded letters. "I always loved your mother's handwriting. Did you know she took a calligraphy class in high school?"

"Is that where you two met?"

"My mother forced me to take the same class. We had gotten into a fight over it because she insisted it was an important skill for a man to learn in my father's company." Noel laid the individual sheets on the heat register.

He pulled a wallet from his back pocket. His fingers ruffled through papers or bills, stopping at the item he had been searching for. Noel unfolded a faded photograph. "We were inseparable."

In the picture, a young couple snuggled on a blanket that had schoolbooks spread about. It showed the historical Saint Aurora high school in the background.

Mom's facial expression was one I had never seen before, pure radiant happiness. The kind associated with being in love. This differed from loving me. I understood, now, why she never mentioned Noel. He had crushed her heart. A lump formed in my throat.

"Would you like to have this?" Noel asked softly.

A whisper pushed itself past the lump in my throat. "Thanks."

"You can still call me Noel. I don't expect you to call me dad, since I wasn't around when you were a kid. But I hope you'll allow me in your life."

I pointed at the letters. The wet spot was now shriveled into a lumpy light brown stain. How could I have been so careless? I should have read them in bed instead. At least they'd still be legible. "They're dry."

"So they are. May I try reading them?"

I shrugged.

The dried blur was no more legible than the wet words. Noel lifted the first page. His eyes flitted across the page, and at the end, he cleared his throat. "My darling pumpkin?"

"Mom's nickname because I was born around Halloween. She said I was the chubbiest baby she had ever seen."

Noel laughed.

Though I shouldn't have smiled, I did. It was a nickname I had hated but now found sentimental. The lump squeezed against my throat. I missed her. I missed how she greeted me, whether it was on the phone or in person.

"Meredith always picked the most terrible nicknames. She would call me honey buns. Every time she called me that, I'd argue with her about it until the early hours of the morning." Noel shook his head with a smile. "As much as I hated it, I missed it when she left."

"Me too."

Noel flipped the page. After he had finished reading, he collected the other loose papers and stacked them together. His eyes glistened against the sunlight. "You don't need to read these."

"Why?"

"My letter is like yours. She worried about you being alone and wanted me there to take her place, except teach you about family."

"Can I read yours?"

The folded envelope I had seen Noel pull from his pocket that day in the cemetery emerged in his hands once again. He allowed me to take it. His letter showed signs of cracking and the handwriting so well-worn it was faint. Her words were ingrained within his mind, so that his eyes didn't need to see the words whenever he read the letter.

The first line was more smudged than the rest. I guessed what she had written in its grayed space. Honey Buns. I replaced the letter inside the cracked envelope. "She wrote it too, didn't she?"

Noel nodded, returning the letter to its home.

"I don't need to read the letters because I know what she wrote. Since coming here… I've felt things I've never had before, a kinship with people."

Noel raised his arms shoulder length apart, and I found myself within them. He caressed my hair. "I believe your mom's angel intervened that day we met outside the hospital."

TWENTY

Strands of hair sprang loose from its bun. I undid it and sighed. My thick wavy hair never cooperated. Noel had insisted that Christian and I attend the shelter's Christmas ball tonight because he wanted help to secure donations.

Did Noel plan on introducing me tonight as his daughter? I wasn't ready for that yet.

I twisted my hair and jabbed in the bobby pins. As I studied it in the mirror, the French twist tumbled. "Damn it," I muttered.

"Do you need help?" Chloe asked.

Where did she come from? I blinked. "Yes, please."

"Your green dress complements your red hair." Chloe plucked the remaining bobby pins from my unruly hair.

I smoothed my hands over the satiny material. Noel had shown up with it in a box yesterday and given it to me. He wouldn't let me repay him, saying, "Just be your charming self at the ball."

Had he known what he was asking of me? Noel wanted me, the girl who couldn't even attend the hospital's

Christmas party, to go to a ball and ask people for money, and not just people, rich people. My stomach churned.

"I'm finished," said Chloe.

I examined myself in the vanity mirror. Words couldn't describe how she had tamed my wild hair. Braids swept upward into a fancy updo. "How?"

Chloe smirked. "I used to help my mom do my sisters' hair."

"Wow, it's beautiful. I hate doing my hair. I usually throw it into a messy bun and call it good most days."

"Christian sent me. He and Noel are waiting for your grand entrance."

"Thanks to you, I'm ready."

Both men stared upon my arrival in the lobby. "Beautiful," said Noel. He nudged Christian forward. "Give her an arm."

The ball gown swooshed in a gentle rocking pattern. Christian and I met in the middle. He did not extend a hand or an elbow but presented a kiss on my cheek. His candy orange breath tickled my ear. "You look dazzling tonight."

His shoulder-length black hair was slicked back, the first time I had ever seen it tidied. The black tuxedo and bowtie highlighted his blue eyes. Our gaze locked on one another. "So do you," I replied.

"May I escort you?" Christian extended an elbow.

"Yes."

Noel smiled. He bowed and held the door for us.

It was like living a fairy tale. However, fairy tales did not include a limo driver checking underneath the hood. He wiped his hands on a dirty rag. "I think it's the alternator."

I released Christian's elbow.

Christian shimmied off his jacket and draped it over his arm. "Hold onto this for me?"

"What are you doing?" I asked.

"Helping." He loosened his bowtie then unbuttoned his cuffs, rolling them back.

"I called the office and it'll be several hours before another driver is available," said the limo driver.

"Noel…" Christian tossed him a set of keys. "You and Holly take my truck and I'll meetcha there."

"But your speech," said Noel.

"I'll make it in time."

The two men exchanged looks. "I promise," said Christian.

"I swear, every year it gets closer and closer to your speech time and it makes me nervous."

Christian patted Noel's shoulder. "Have I ever missed it, old man? Now, get going."

Noel and I walked away. Christian's jacket flopped, providing a reminder he needed it later. I turned around. "Your jacket."

"Keep it for me."

The driver entered the limo and left the driver's door open. Christian peered under the hood. "Start it."

"Nothing," said the driver. He joined Christian in examining the car's inner parts.

The situation interested me. I had never observed men working on a car before. They talked with one another and brainstormed ideas for the limo's death. Christian must have worked on machinery at the tree farm.

Noel tugged my arm. "We need to go."

At Christian's pickup, Noel opened the passenger door. I gathered up my skirts and found I couldn't fit through the opening. Several minutes passed. I re-adjusted my skirts until it cleared the doorway. Inside, my gown puffed up like cramming in the wrong puzzle piece.

Noel chuckled. "I should have bought you a smaller dress."

I manipulated the material, flattening it enough for a seatbelt. "If this is my carriage, then my fairy god-mother failed," I mumbled.

I gasped. Sparkly crystal snowflakes dangled from the ceiling at various lengths with a soft blue backlight. Noel's simplistic fundraiser ball had morphed into a Christmas wonderland.

White flocked Christmas trees scattered about the monstrous ballroom. Silver ribbons twirled around each tree, combining in a fancy bow atop the peak. They gleamed against the lit clear lights. "One... two..." I counted the different-sized trees but soon stopped after ten.

"Do you approve?" Noel whispered.

"It's beautiful."

"We have an hour before Christian speaks. Look for him while you're mingling with the guests."

"What do I say? Something like, hey, the shelter needs money, so give us a huge donation?"

A roaring laugh came from behind. "Oh, Noel, where did you find her? I like her," said a man holding a slender cane.

"Mr. Nelson, I present to you Holly Bradford."

His dull gray eyes squinted, blending into his wrinkled face. "Auburn hair, eh? Reminds me what yours used to be like, Noel."

"'Tis a memory now."

A waitress lowered a tray containing wine glasses.

I selected white wine. The bitter taste swirled around in my mouth. I swallowed it. It was all I could do to keep from gagging. Noel and Mr. Nelson sipped theirs and reminisced about their glory days.

Red cloths covered circular tables large enough to seat a dozen. The two men paid little attention as I made my way towards one. Three burning candles sat on a wood slab. I sniffed. Was that pine?

"The decorators did a pretty job this year, didn't they?" A blonde woman stood next to a chair.

"How can the shelter afford all this?"

"Sponsors." The woman loomed closer, raising a gloved hand. "I'm Gabriella Thornton."

A glimpse of the abandoned NICU baby flashed in my mind. Had someone adopted her? The unanswered question interwove along with other questions about the little fighter.

Gabriella waited with an extended hand.

"I'm sorry. Your name reminded me of someone." I accepted her handshake. "Holly Bradford. Thornton… do you know a Dylan Thornton?"

"He's my ex-husband, and the father of our two boys."

"What are you doing here?"

"Noel invited me. He invites all the families." She smoothed her dress. "How is he?"

I shrugged. "Ashamed. Hurt."

"Our boys keep asking about him, but he won't return our letters or calls."

"We talked a few days ago, and he said he'd call."

"Sometimes at night I see him lurking about outside our house, watching us."

I grabbed ahold of her hand. "Come celebrate Christmas at the shelter."

"Do… do you think Dylan would allow us?" Tears hovered around the edges of her eyes but did not fall.

"I'll talk to him."

"Thank you. The boys miss him so much."

People continued arriving through the entrance, though none were Christian. Gabriella looked in the direction I kept staring at. "Looking for someone?"

"Christian."

"You mean Dr. Hunt from the infirmary?"

"Yes, our limo had engine problems, and he stayed behind with the driver to fix it. His speech starts soon."

Amongst the crowd, Noel spoke with another gentleman. He met my gaze and turned his head towards the doorway.

"Maybe—"

"I'm sorry, please excuse me." I started for the entrance.

In the crowd, I shared smiles and mutters of apologies.

Noel met me in the foyer. He raised his hand and uncovered an expensive looking wristwatch. "We've got less than five minutes."

"What are we going to do?"

"Go to the coatroom and get Christian's jacket. Keep looking for him. I'm going to the stage." Noel navigated through the crowd.

People stopped him several times, and he gave an apologetic smile before continuing. At last, I tore myself away from studying my father.

The woman servant in the coatroom remembered me. "You want his jacket?"

"Yes, he's running late."

She disappeared into a room containing what appeared to be hundreds of coats. I tapped my foot. Each passing second, she spent searching seemed like hours.

And no Christian. What would Noel do?

TWENTY-ONE

Noel took the microphone. "Welcome to the fifth annual fundraiser ball for the Reed Homeless Shelter for Veterans. I want to thank everyone for supporting our cause…"

Someone touched my shoulder, startling me. "I told ya I would make it," said Christian. He took his jacket and shrugged into it. On his scarred cheek was a visible black smudge.

I grabbed a cloth napkin off a table.

Before I tried wiping it, he clasped my wrist. "Don't, you'll ruin it. It's likely grease."

"You can't go up there with a dirty face."

"Fine." Christian released my wrist.

I rubbed the grease spot using the cloth's edge until no remnants showed. "All clean." When I stepped back, I held my breath at how close our faces had been. Our eyes danced with one another in silence.

Christian broke it. "Thanks. The speech."

We moved in the same direction at the same time. "Sorry," I mumbled, moving aside.

Christian made his way across the ballroom. At the last table, he poured a glass of water and brought it with him on stage.

Noel finished his speech by introducing Christian. The crowd clapped and whistled as the two men exchanged handshakes and private words.

Christian stood at the podium, tall and rigid, the way he might have stood when at attention in the military. He took a sip of water.

"Good evening. My name is Doctor Christian Hunt, and I am here tonight to share my story. By the time I retired from the Army, I had become an addict in search of my next escape from reality. Eventually, my addiction stripped away the easy life I had, and I landed on the streets.

One rainy afternoon, I stumbled upon an unconscious man and despite my efforts, he died of a drug overdose before the ambulance arrived. That man turned out to be Noel's son, Reed…"

In the crowd, a familiar face stared in my direction. Mr. Israelson? It can't be. He smiled. I weaved through the throng and stopped where I had seen him. A man stood there, but it was not him. I spun around, searching.

"Hi, Holly," Mr. Israelson whispered in my ear. He held two glasses of red wine, extending one. "Wine?"

"Mr. Israelson. What are you doing here?" My fingers curled around the stem. I took a sip, but the wine did not alleviate my dry mouth.

"Call me Ric." He raised my hand to his lips and kissed it.

Was he hitting on me?

Mr. Israelson joined in with the audience's clapping. I had missed the end of Christian's speech.

A quartet resumed playing Christmas music. From the stage, Christian peered at me with a crooked smile. He disappeared into the crowd.

"Dance with me?" asked Mr. Israelson. He took my glass and set it on a passing waiter's tray, then led me to the dance floor.

"Relax, you're too tense." He instructed through a turn.

I mis-stepped and stumbled. "Are you going to tell me why you are here?"

"Noel invited me." Mr. Israelson whispered, "I'm—"

Christian interjected. "May I cut in?"

"Sure." Mr. Israelson stepped aside and took his leave.

Christian placed my hand inside his, and the other rested on my waist. "Are you ready?"

"I'm a terrible dancer," I warned.

"Silent Night" began.

I stiffened upon hearing my mother's favorite song. Noel must have requested it. Don't be silly, it's a popular Christmas carol.

"This was her favorite song, wasn't it?"

"Yeah, tell me about Noel and the shelter. Like how did it get started?"

"You don't know?"

"Know what?"

Christian and I twirled. "When I met him, he was a billionaire. He still is, but all the money is spent on the shelter and his other projects."

"How?"

"He didn't tell you anything? You should talk to him about these things."

"Please."

"His real estate investment has made him wealthy. It's what gives him the connections around town for donations."

The song ended. Christian led me off the dance floor and to an isolated spot behind a group of Christmas trees. "The police accused me of murdering Reed. While I was in prison waiting for the trial, Noel visited. At first, I wouldn't let him, but he was persistent."

"What happened?"

"He hired a lawyer and got me off. Together we created the shelter for veterans."

Through the tree branches, Noel conversed with an elderly lady wearing a gold gown. I should have guessed. At the courthouse, he had mentioned money doesn't bring happiness.

I faced Christian. "I spoke with Dylan's ex-wife earlier. She said that Noel invites all the families to take part in the ball. Why?"

"Come with me."

We walked the length of the ballroom along the outer edges and exited into the foyer. "Where are we going?" I asked.

"You'll see."

The woman, who had given me Christian's jacket earlier, gave a slight smile and a single nod.

I hesitated. Too many movies I had watched showed a couple using the coatroom for wild, passionate sex.

"Are you coming?" asked Christian.

"Uh…"

Christian tilted his head to the side and studied me. He chuckled. "I'm afraid not. There's too many people around."

Warmth crept across my face and chest. I said nothing and followed him inside. A clear box rested on a table in the center of the room. Colored envelopes with names scrawled across them filled the locked box.

"They're messages," said Christian.

"I don't understand."

"It's why Noel invites the families. They write letters, and he delivers them."

"Doesn't that violate their privacy at the shelter?"

"Noel asks permission. Many times, our tenants don't know how to reconcile with their families. So once a year, Noel opens that gateway for them by providing this letterbox."

Tears dammed up within. The pictures in Noel's desk drawers... they were proof that his methods worked.

Christian caressed my face. "I guess you could say Noel is like Santa Claus. His miracles include mending people and families."

"Why do you call him old man?"

"It's an inside joke between us. It started during our first visit when we had gotten into an argument. I said something about he's nothing but an old man — I don't remember the whole disagreement." Christian stifled a laugh.

"He's like a father to you, I gather?"

"More like a pain in my ass sometimes."

"I'm his daughter."

"I know."

"What? How—"

Christian grasped my hands and pulled me closer. His lips swooped on mine. I pressed harder, wanting to devour his orange candy flavored mouth. A tingle transformed my skin into something alive. Our breathing quickened.

I pushed away but left my hands against his chest.

His lips curled into a half-grin. "Was it so bad, making out in a coatroom?"

TWENTY-TWO

When the last patient of the day left, I locked the infirmary door. Behind me, a plastic bag rattled.

Christian plopped his favorite candy in his mouth. He wiped his sugar-coated fingers against his scrubs and wrote something on his clipboard. Only one candy orange slice remained in the bag.

I snagged it and sat on the exam table. "I got the last one," I teased, waving it back and forth.

"Hey, that's mine." Christian went to snatch it out of my hand, but I shoved it in my mouth with a smirk.

I tucked it against my right cheek and spoke around it. "Guess you'll have to get it out of my mouth."

"Is that a challenge?" asked Christian, giving his usual half-grin.

"May—"

Christian covered my lips with his sticky fingers caressing my jaw. Someone rapped at the door multiple times. He groaned. "Leave it, they'll go away."

I giggled and tugged at his shirt.

Before his lips reached mine, the raps grew louder. A muffled voice shouted, "I know you're in there, Holly."

"Let them in," I said with a sigh.

Christian unlocked the door and opened it.

Dylan emerged through the doorway and halted, his feet shoulder-width apart. His eyes narrowed. "What gives you the right to interfere in my business?"

He found out. I swallowed. Dylan wasn't supposed to find out.

"What are you talking about?" Christian asked.

"Answer me, Holly," said Dylan.

Christian stared at him then me. "What is he talking about?"

"Tell him how you invited my ex-wife and sons here for Christmas."

"You promised you would call." I crossed my arms.

"No, I said I might."

"How did you find out, anyway?" I asked.

Dylan removed a crumpled letter from his pants pocket and threw it, the balled-up paper landing at my feet. "Gabriella wrote me."

"Your sons miss you. They want to see you. Don't you get it?"

"Their dad is nothing more than a bum."

"Who cares if you're homeless? You're still providing for them."

"Stay away from me." Dylan whirled around and limped out into the hallway.

I picked up the tossed letter and unraveled the mashed ball. It crinkled as I flattened it. Inside contained two letters written by his sons. Gabriella must have slipped her note in with their sons' letters after speaking with me at the ball.

"You okay?" asked Christian.

"He's upset with me." I faced him. "I thought seeing his sons was what he wanted."

"I can't believe you did that. You're a meddler and you can't help yourself, can you?" Christian shook his head with a half-smile.

He was right. I still hadn't learned my lesson after our argument over Chloe. My feelings remained bottled within, wrapped tightly for fear of exposing my vulnerability. Christian saw it, and he still stayed.

The past three weeks, he had shared clues of his, so did Chloe and Dylan. Even the women in my support group had. They all wanted someone to listen instead of fixing their problems.

I cleared my throat. "Can I talk to you?"

"About?"

"Never mind."

Christian towered over me, resting his hands on my shoulders. "Talk to me," he whispered.

"When I—" I nibbled my bottom lip and released it. "I never understood PTSD until I was abducted. Wanting to die to escape the pain... I don't know how you, everybody here, and the soldiers overseas survive every single day."

"After I came home, my enemy was time. It was easy over there because saving lives consumed my mind."

"Was that why you turned to drugs?"

"We all numb ourselves somehow. Drugs, booze, sex, denial..."

I returned to my seat on the exam table, and Christian sat on a stool. "I can't sleep," I admitted.

"What happens in your nightmares?"

"I'm blinded by the floodlights, then I hear a door slam, like an echo."

"What else?"

"Men talking."

Christian rolled his chair, stopping in front of my legs. "I want you to see Amy."

"Amy… the gal that used to run the support group?"

"She's an expert in helping with PTSD, and she owes me a favor. I'll call her."

"You were there."

"In the nightmare?"

I shook my head. "When I was hallucinating, you were there."

"I guessed."

"How?"

"At the warehouse, you asked me if I was real." Christian lowered his voice. "I think about you too."

"I—"

"Let's not worry about figuring it out. For now, can't we enjoy each other's company?"

I folded his hand over mine. "I'd like that."

"You should go finish talking to Dylan."

Dylan was where I suspected, in the courtyard. Christian stood with me in front of the door that led outside as I studied Dylan's hunched figure on the bench. The letters crackled when I smoothed them again.

"Do you want me to go with you?" asked Christian.

I shook my head. "I need to do this alone."

"I'll wait for you here."

Snowflakes fluttered in the air, unsure where to land and clinging to anything they could. They melted when they landed against my exposed skin. The breeze made me shiver. I should have gotten my coat before I came here. I pressed on.

Dylan turned his gaze on me. "What do you want?"

"I wanted to apologize. When I talked to your ex-wife, my emotions clouded my judgment, and I wanted to fix this problem."

"Is that my sons' letters?"

"Yeah." I held them out. "Did you read them?"

"No."

I snatched back the letters that hovered within inches of his fingers. "Why not?"

Dylan shrugged.

"Dear Dad. I asked Santa…" My voice cracked at his son's written words. "to bring you home for Christmas."

"Why are you doing this?"

"Because I care about you. You may have chosen us to be your family, but don't ignore the one you were given."

"May I have my letters?"

I extended them again, then jerked them out of his reach. "Are you gonna read them?"

"Fine," Dylan sighed. "I promise I will read them."

"You better." I allowed him to reclaim his letters.

Dylan rubbed his thumb over his son's handwriting. "His writing is getting good."

"That's what happens when you're gone."

"Ouch, that hurt."

"Why don't you come inside? I'll make hot chocolate and we can talk where it's warmer."

Dylan rose. "Thanks, but um… I need to call my ex-wife."

TWENTY-THREE

CHRISTMAS EVE

The wind howled outside. It sought to wiggle itself into any cracks that it could find in our sanctuary. Snow hurled against the windows in retaliation, making it difficult to see out. The storm snuck past the shelter's doors whenever they opened. A steady stream of people searched for an evening haven, which we obliged.

By six o'clock, the weather reports estimated ten inches of snow had fallen. It continued snowing.

Lights flickered. Noel had reassured us earlier that the backup generators were prepped and ready to go if the electricity went out. He also waived the shelter's rules for tonight.

People loitered in any available space they could find. Christian and I scoured through closets for blankets, passing them out as we passed through rooms. A piano key sounded. Other instruments soon tuned to the correct note.

Please don't play "Silent Night," I repeated silently.

The opening to the song began. I glanced around the lobby, but people continued talking over the music. My heart thumped until it was all I could hear. The chorus slithered from my mouth.

One by one people joined in and the song crescendoed. When it ended, the lump that usually appeared in my throat never came. Mom would have loved the caroling I had encouraged on this stormy Christmas Eve.

A loud explosion came from outside, followed by the crowd's startled gasps. Darkness settled upon the shelter. The emergency lights flickered on, then powered off. Something was wrong.

The small band continued playing. People resumed singing along with the Christmas songs.

A callused hand clasped mine. "We need to go to the basement and see why the generator isn't working," Christian spoke near my ear.

A beam of light flashed at us.

Christian turned on his pocket-sized flashlight and shined it toward the incoming light. It was Chloe.

Chloe elbowed her way through the crowd. "I can help," she shouted.

"Follow us." Christian pointed the light at the hallway we were to use.

We navigated through the throng of people. If the shelter had a capacity limit, the amount of people in here had long since exceeded it. The crowd became sparse the farther we walked down the hallway.

Christian let go of my hand. "Chloe, shine your light on the door."

His keys jingled as he unlocked the basement door. Christian twisted the knob and pushed, grunting at its stickiness. He heaved his body weight against the door. "Come on. Open."

The door groaned. Christian slammed against it again. At last the door opened. Chloe's light illuminated a set of steep stairs.

"You go first," said Christian.

Chloe gasped. She grasped the railing.

"Is it the baby?" I asked.

"I'm fine." Chloe released her grip. "Let's get this done so we have light."

Christian and I followed but said nothing.

Chloe stopped on the bottom step and blew out another sharp exhale. When the pain must have subsided, she continued onward to the generator. "In my experience the carburetor is gummed up or bad fuel was put in it. You got a ten millimeter deep-well socket and a three-eighths inch ratchet in there?" She examined the generator, moving her light at different angles. "Oh, and a flat-head screwdriver."

"Yeah," said Christian. He went to a tool chest that stood waist-high on him. Tools rattled as drawers slid open and shut. The requested tools in one hand and the flashlight in the other, he asked, "How far apart are your contractions?"

"I'm not in labor. Now give me the damn tools." Chloe snatched the ratchet and socket. It clicked as she went to work on the bolts. She puffed, stopping.

Christian removed a cover that led to the generator's bowels. The spotlight skimmed inside it. "Looks dry. Do you want to try starting fluid?"

"Not now." Chloe groaned. Her hand flew to her belly. "The baby is coming."

"Now?" I asked.

Chloe leaned against the wall. The light angled on a wet spot on the floor. "My water broke."

"Help me lay her down on the floor." Christian divested his sweater. He gave it and the flashlight to me. "Place this underneath her. She'll need a clean spot to deliver."

"Deliver?" Chloe panted. "Here?"

"With the storm, the ambulance won't make it."

"Oh no, no, no. The infirmary."

"Chloe, you can do this." Christian tugged down her pants. "We can do this." He murmured more soothing words like he was calming down a child.

Chloe whimpered. She lifted a foot and allowed Christian to push aside her underwear and pants.

Christian eased her into a delivering position, and I placed the sweatshirt underneath her butt.

"Stay here with her. I am going to the laundry room and gathering supplies."

"Don't leave me," pleaded Chloe.

"Holly will be with you." Christian disappeared farther into the basement until we couldn't see him anymore.

Chloe screamed. She squeezed hard, nearly folding my hand in half like a sandwich. When she relaxed, I massaged the pain. "I'm sorry," she said through clenched teeth. "I hate this."

Water trickled somewhere. A bang thunked against what might have been a sink. A bleach aroma permeated in the air, melding with the generator's stench. Christian must be sterilizing his hands.

"That reeks." Chloe crinkled her nose.

"How long have you been having contractions?"

"Since early this morning." Chloe bunched the sweater in her fists. Her voice came out strained. "They're getting closer."

"Wait for Christian."

"I'm here." Christian set down a stack of towels. It was more than we needed. He took the top one and used a knife to tear off a strip. The single strip was laid back on the towel. "Be ready with a towel."

"I will."

Christian draped a towel over Chloe's hips and upper legs. "How far apart are your contractions?"

"Two to three minutes," Chloe replied.

"I'm gonna see if the baby turned." Christian checked and muttered, "Damn it. Still breech."

The situation soured. All the doctors I had worked with, in the past, performed C-sections on breech positions. The basement was not an optimal place for one. "What do you want to do?" I asked.

"Deliver. It's too late to try and turn the baby."

Chloe shook her head furiously. "I can't do this."

"Yes, you can, because you are a survivor. You can do this, I know you can do this," said Christian. "Now, this is important. When I tell you to stop pushing, you stop."

I studied Christian's face. For a dangerous birthing position, he appeared calm. Former Army Doctor. This obstacle must have seemed minor compared to what he had seen overseas.

"Holly, I want you to stand beside me. Be ready to do what I ask."

I complied.

"Now push, Chloe."

Chloe bore down, stifling her screams.

Soon a tiny butt presented itself. Christian raised his voice, "Stop." He manipulated the baby until he freed its legs. "On your next push, I'm gonna twist the baby to ease its shoulders and arms out."

Chloe pushed again. Her stifled screams grew louder, but she remained tight-lipped.

Christian swiveled the baby's body with his large hand. His other slipped inside the birth canal. The shoulders and arms emerged while Christian's hand remained in the canal. "Holly, push down on her uterus with a fist."

I assumed the position and waited.

"Now."

I pressed down with all the force I could muster. Chloe's screams pierced my ears. The seconds stretched.

"Towel," said Christian.

I breathed a sigh of relief. Christian had done it. I wrapped the towel around the baby and held her.

Christian tied off the umbilical cord and separated mother and child. He attended to Chloe.

I rubbed the newborn and she let out a cry. "It's a girl."

Chloe said nothing.

I cleaned the baby and swaddled her with several more towels. For added warmth, I snuggled the newborn against my body. "Chloe, would you like to hold your daughter?"

"I don't have a daughter," said Chloe in a glacial tone. She turned her head away from us.

Twenty-Four

In the night, it quit snowing. Saint Aurora received around sixteen inches of snow, leaving behind a white ocean in its wake. After an early morning start, Christian and volunteers finished clearing the shelter's circular driveway. Red lights flashed in the distance, reflecting off the fresh snow.

It had been hours since Christian had called the ambulance. I glanced from the window to a sleeping Chloe and baby. My throat tightened at what we had done to her. We had no choice. It was force her to breastfeed or let the baby die. Every two hours since the baby's birth, it had been a battle with Chloe to nurse her.

Someone rapped on the door. "The ambulance's here," said Christian.

The paramedics bundled up Chloe and her newborn. They rolled the gurney down the hallway and out the front door to the waiting ambulance.

I shivered as they loaded the gurney. Chloe would never forgive us for what we did.

A glove rested upon my arm. "Let's go inside," said Christian. He wrapped an arm around my shoulders and guided me inside the lobby.

We continued past the sleeping crowd. In the kitchen, Eric stood in front of the coffeemaker while Noel read an old newspaper at the island.

"Merry Christmas." Noel folded the paper. "Did Chloe and the baby get off to the hospital?"

"Yeah, the paramedics said they'd call when they got Chloe checked in," Christian replied.

Glass shattered. Eric swore as he knelt to the floor. He ranted and raved under his breath while picking up the broken pieces of a cup.

"Eric, is everything okay?" asked Christian.

"I'm fine." Eric threw the shards into the garbage can. He grabbed a broom and swept the floor.

I stepped forward, and he flinched. "I can finish, if you want to get yourself another cup of coffee."

"No, I'll do it."

"Holly." Christian gestured at the clock on the wall. "We need to change into our costumes."

I removed two mugs from the cabinet. "I don't know about you, but I need coffee."

"Now. We'll get coffee later."

I grumbled, leaving the cups on the countertop.

"You ready to play Mrs. Claus?"

"Only if Mrs. Claus gets coffee," I mumbled.

Christian chuckled.

We tiptoed through the sleeping mass in the hallway and lobby. Christian opened the door leading to the stairs. "I don't trust the generator enough to take the elevator."

"Where are we going?"

"My room."

I remained quiet.

"There's no time for that," he teased. "Everyone will wake soon."

Heat worked its way across my skin. I was sure my face was redder than Rudolph's nose. We would have done it that day in the infirmary, if Dylan hadn't interrupted. My heartbeat quickened at how close we'd been.

After two flights of stairs, we entered the hallway leading to Christian's room. I trailed behind him as we walked to his room. It would be the first time I got an unobstructed view of his room. I hadn't been back since he kissed me as a distraction. A tingle skittered across my arms and up the back of my neck.

Christian swung open the door to his room. "Ladies first."

I entered. It seemed strange to return here three weeks later. Christian's room was unlike Deacon's dorm room in our college years. The room was tidy, and the walls free from decorations. A neat pile of red and white clothes sat folded on the bed.

"You okay?" asked Christian.

"I was remembering how we met."

"You've changed."

"Have I?" I slumped on the bed. "I still want a baby."

"You and Deacon never got pregnant?"

"We tried." I squeezed my eyelids closed, afraid to see his reaction. "The doctors diagnosed me with unexplained infertility."

"Even if a woman gets pregnant, it's not a guarantee."

"What do you mean?"

"Look at my wife. She and our child died." The bed squeaked under his weight. "Open your eyes."

I did.

His blue eyes bored into mine. "Things still happen like a miscarriage, stillborn, or the child is born with a disease. You still can't protect 'em after they're born."

"I want to leave a legacy behind," I whispered.

"You have, by being you."

"Thanks…"

"Chloe got to you, didn't she?"

The costume's red and white blurred. I traced the seam along the bottom of what I presumed to be Santa's coat.

"Remember what I told you that first day? In here, we're all fighting a war inside us. Chloe is too."

"You're right. It's hard to not want what someone else has."

Christian sorted through the clothes and raised a dress. "Now how about we go spread Christmas cheer to some folks?" He rose, holding the dress against his body. "Do you think I'd make a good Mrs. Claus?"

"Hm… you're missing something." I snatched the wig off his bed and placed it on his head. A fit of giggles escaped. "There, now your outfit is complete."

"That's the Holly I like seeing." Christian laid the dress back on the bed. He took off the wig and put it on me. "Let's go celebrate Christmas with our family."

On our way to the infirmary, Christian and I laughed while we reminisced about the morning's celebration. He was right about spreading Christmas cheer. It had lifted my own dampened spirits with giving gifts to the others. I smiled as I recalled their reactions.

There was one that clutched at my heartstrings, Dylan's. Tears of joy had claimed him victim when he embraced his two boys.

Christian intruded on my memories. "Hey, I'll meet ya in the infirmary. I need to use the restroom first."

"You're breaking the escort rule." I batted my eyelashes.

"You'll be fine. Everyone is downstairs, sitting around the tree and celebrating."

"Yeah, what could happen in five minutes?"

Christian kissed my cheek. "I'll hurry." He pushed the bathroom door, disappearing inside.

I continued farther down the hallway and slowed upon the sight of broken glass on the tiled floor. The infirmary door was ajar. A shadow lurked in the room, speaking gibberish.

"Hello?" I asked.

The person responded with nonsensical sentences.

Glass tinkled under my boots. I crept through the doorway and flipped on the light switch. "Are you hurt?"

The man didn't move. The incessant ramblings continued.

I eased forward. "I'd like to help you."

My foot kicked the wheel on a rolling table. It crashed to the floor, causing a reverberated clang.

The man spun around.

"Eric? What are you doing in here?"

"Get away," Eric shouted. Something metal glinted in his hand. He jerked forward and slashed at me.

I careened back, the knife barely missing. "It's Holly."

Eric didn't answer.

We circled each other, and he struck again. I sucked in a scream, afraid it would worsen his PTSD episode. Blood dripped from the gash on my forearm. I forced a steady voice. "I'm not here to hurt you."

Eric brought up the knife and sliced through the air.

Without thinking, I sprinted at him, like a football player ready to tackle.

Eric staggered backwards. The knife hit the floor with a clink.

We scrambled for the knife, reaching for it at the same time. I yanked, but his grip was too tight.

Items dropped to the floor as we continued fighting each other for power over the knife. The blade bit into my palm. I screamed.

Eric wrested it away from my slippery grasp and shoved me. The back of my head collided with the floor, jolting a sharp pain across my skull. "Die. Must die," he chanted as he straddled my waist.

"Get off of me," I shrieked. I pummeled him anywhere I could connect a fist with.

The blade hovered above my chest. Eric lowered the knife. "Die. Must die."

I clamped my hands over his and resisted the downward motion. My muscles burned. It was a losing battle, but I needed to hold on until Christian saved me. The knife inched closer. "Stop it, Eric." I grunted. "It's Holly."

The point pricked my skin. I cried out, "Christian."

Eric jabbed the knife in farther, stopping when the hilt jammed against my chest. He tore out the knife.

I gasped. Time ebbed in a slow motion.

Eric clambered into the corner, leaving behind a trail of blood droplets.

I lay frozen in an expanding blood pool. My hands trembled over the stab wound. Warmth mingled with coldness on my skin from blood soaking in Mrs. Claus' dress. The vibrations of my frantic heartbeat coursed throughout my body, rendering it nearly impossible to breathe.

A clank hit the floor. Eric curled into a fetal position and rocked back and forth. "I'm sorry. I'm so sorry," he reiterated nonstop.

"Holly." Christian's voice stretched out my name like he was far away.

My mouth snapped opened and closed, but I couldn't speak. I wheezed. Mom's favorite Christmas song began playing. The chorus grew louder. A familiar soprano voice sang above the others. I never imagined that "Silent Night" would be my death song.

A metallic taste developed inside my mouth. Blood. I can't believe I'm going to die on Mom's favorite day of the year. Garbled voices surrounded me.

Blurred faces bobbed in and out near my face. I closed my eyes. It was getting harder to stay. My body moved on something hard. Is it a gurney? Someone pried my eyelid open and an angel's halo shone. "Are you here to take me to heaven?"

The angel laughed. "No pumpkin, it's not time."

I squinted. "Mom?" Wetness renewed itself with each blink. "Is that you?"

"Hi, Holly, my sweet girl." Her blurry glow dissolved until the Mom I remembered materialized.

"Mom," I shouted as I embraced her. Something shocked me. I stepped back and held out my arms. It happened again. My body jerked. "What's happening?"

"I don't have a lot of time. A surprise is waiting for you at the hospital. One last gift from me." She smiled.

"Wait, Mom. Don't go."

Mom hugged me and gave a kiss on my forehead. "I was so blessed to have you for a daughter. I love you."

"I love you too."

She vanished.

TWENTY-FIVE

My eyelids forced the grit to release its hold. Everything blurred. I squeezed my eyes shut and reopened them. Where am I? I stirred to a more comfortable position, wincing at the pain in my chest. Eric. Knife.

I glimpsed at the taped IV in my hand. Hospital. Which one? Christian lay sleeping with his head beside my hip and an arm across my legs. Answers. I need answers. I rasped a whisper of his name.

Christian did not respond.

My fingers stretched to reach his hand. It was too far away. I grunted inside at how something close seemed difficult. Footsteps padded in my room.

"Christian, she's awake," said Noel.

Christian's piercing blue eyes glanced up towards mine. He kissed my cheek. "I'm glad you stayed," he said in a low voice. "I only just gotcha."

A squeak came from behind him. A bassinet seemed to be sitting there, in which Noel picked up a squirming baby girl. "Meet your daughter, Faith Noelle."

Had he named her after Mom's middle name? Faith's name held a deeper meaning somehow, especially after seeing Mom.

Noel held her closer. Her little fingers curled around mine and tears sprang to my eyes. Chloe. She had talked about giving her baby up for adoption. She wanted me? The tears spilled.

"I'm gonna inform your doctor you're awake." Christian stretched with a yawn.

Noel hummed while he walked and rocked the baby around the room. It was the same tune Mom had hummed throughout my life, her favorite song. He stopped singing. "Chloe's gone."

I stared.

"She checked herself out."

"Where?"

"Chloe talked about turning herself in for desertion."

Christian returned, carrying a water mug. The ice rattled as he brought the straw to my lips. "Drink."

The cold liquid did not soothe my throat. "Thank you," I said hoarsely. "Eric?"

"He's been committed at the psychiatric hospital." Christian set down the mug. "Holly, I'm sorry. I should have talked to him in the kitchen then maybe he wouldn't have stabbed you." He buried his face within his hands.

"N-n-no."

"If you're at fault, then I am too," said Noel.

Baby Faith squirmed, her squeaks turning into cries. Noel patted her tiny behind and tried to settle her, but she wasn't having it. A familiar face appeared with a bottle in her hand.

"Marnie? Is that you?"

"Hi Holly, how are you feeling?" Marnie smiled.

"Sore. I thought you were let go."

"Saint Aurora hired me." Marnie stopped at the edge of my bed. "From what I hear, you're lucky. I brought Faith's bottle, it's time for her feeding."

"Would you like to try feeding your daughter?" asked Noel.

"Can I?"

Marnie set the bottle on the bedside. She adjusted the incline of the bed and shifted my pillows around until she was satisfied.

Noel let her take the baby from him.

"Here's your mama, little one," said Marnie. She positioned the baby below my chest, but on my lap. Marnie retrieved the bottle off the table.

The baby's mouth rooted out the nipple and latched on when she found it. Faith suckled on the bottle, making noises of contentment.

I opened my mouth.

"Don't talk." Marnie brought a finger to her lips. "Your daughter is beautiful. Did you hear that Dottie will foster Gabriella?"

I gave a slight shake of my head. "If Gabriella's biological parents don't claim her, Dottie and her husband plan on fostering and later, adopting her."

"How—"

"She's thriving, still in the NICU though. But hey, I have to go do rounds. It was nice seeing you again."

Dottie's fostering? She'd be better than Gabriella's birth parents, who couldn't overcome Gabriella's first challenge. Faith spit out the bottle and fussed.

"May I?" asked Christian. He lifted Faith to his shoulder, cradling her head with one hand and gently caressing her back with the other. Murmurings were whispered in her ear. At last, she burped.

The two of them together filled me with a feeling I had never felt. One that made my heart increase its size until it wanted to burst out of my chest. It was love.

Mom was right. I had a surprise waiting when I came back, one I've wanted for so long. Faith completed the family I had gained. Throughout the month everyone at the shelter had embraced me in my darkest days and became the family I had been searching for most of my life. It was an unexpected gift. I blinked, letting the tears fall.

"Are you all right?" asked Noel, touching my shoulder.

"Just thankful." I removed his hand from my shoulder and gave it a squeeze. "Is it okay if I call you Dad?"

"Of course."

"I saw Mom."

"I bet she was beautiful."

"She wouldn't let me give up."

"I'm glad you stayed. Chloe was worried you wouldn't make it," said Dad.

"Why did she leave me with her daughter?"

"You pushed her to acknowledge her trauma. She said, 'You were the first person to do that.'"

"I have connections, we'll find out where she's at," said Christian. "Would you like your daughter back?"

"Please."

Christian arranged her in my arms and stepped back. His hand slipped inside his coat pocket, rumpling around. He pulled out a cellphone. "You and Faith need a picture together."

"I'd like you and Noel in the picture too."

"I'll go find a nurse," said Noel.

Christian snapped a picture of Faith and me. "You ladies look beautiful."

"I wish Chloe were here."

"We'll find her."

Marnie followed Noel into the room. She took Christian's cellphone and raised the camera. "Say Merry Christmas."

"Merry Christmas." Our voices joined in unison.

The picture done, Marnie looked at the picture and smiled. "You guys make a beautiful family."

"Yes, I've been blessed." These two men had stayed by my side multiple times when I had expected them to leave. Faith's sleeping face matched my long-ago dream. My voice cracked. "This Christmas has been the best I've had in years because I got a family this year."

Tones beeped as Marnie entered something on Christian's phone. When she finished, she returned it to him. "Call me when you and the baby get settled in. I'll throw you a baby shower."

"I'd… I'd like that."

"I'll stop by after my shift and we can visit longer." Marnie waved goodbye.

"Can I see the pictures?" I asked.

Christian stared at his phone. "That's strange. I'll retake the picture of you and Faith."

"Why?"

"I must have gotten the glare of the light or something." Christian showed me his phone.

A light shadow stood beside me, and a streak went behind my back, like an arm. My throat constricted around the forming lump. "Mom," I whispered.

"Do you want me to retake the picture?"

"No, it's perfect. This was Mom's last Christmas gift."

The End

If you enjoyed reading
Her Mother's Last Christmas Gift,
please consider leaving a review.

To follow my author journey,
please consider following me on Facebook at
https://www.facebook.com/authorkyleighmccloud
or by visiting my website at www.kyleighmccloud.com

Acknowledgments

I would like to thank my friends, Karen and Lexee. It was through their encouragement that I finished and published Holly's story.

I also want to thank my loving husband for his patience, wisdom, and putting up listening to Christmas music in the off season. With your love and support, I achieved my dream of being a published author.